HEATH

HEATH

TEXAS BOUDREAU BROTHERHOOD

By

KATHY IVAN

COPYRIGHT

Heath – Original Copyright © December 2020 by Kathy Ivan

Cover by Elizabeth Mackay

Release date: December 2020
Print Edition

All Rights Reserved

HEATH – Texas Boudreau Brotherhood

"In Shiloh Springs, Kathy Ivan has crafted warm, engaging characters that will steal your heart and a mystery that will keep you reading to the very last page." Barb Han, USA TODAY and Publisher's Weekly Bestselling Author

Kathy Ivan's books are addictive, you can't read just one." Susan Stoker, NYT Bestselling Author

BOOKS BY KATHY IVAN

www.kathyivan.com/books.html

TEXAS BOUDREAU BROTHERHOOD
Rafe
Antonio
Brody
Ridge
Lucas
Heath
Shiloh (coming soon)

NEW ORLEANS CONNECTION SERIES
Desperate Choices
Connor's Gamble
Relentless Pursuit
Ultimate Betrayal
Keeping Secrets
Sex, Lies and Apple Pies
Deadly Justice
Wicked Obsession
Hidden Agenda
Spies Like Us
Fatal Intentions
New Orleans Connection Series Box Set: Books 1-3
New Orleans Connection Series Box Set: Books 4-7

Hello Readers,

Welcome to Shiloh Springs, Texas! Don't you just love a small Texas town, where the people are neighborly, the gossip plentiful, and the heroes are...well, heroic, not to mention easy on the eyes! I love everything about Texas, which I why I've made the great state my home for over thirty years. There's no other place like it. From the delicious Tex-Mex food and downhome barbecue, the majestic scenery, and friendly atmosphere, the people and places of the Lone Star state are as unique and colorful as you'll find anywhere.

The Texas Boudreau Brotherhood series centers on a group of foster brothers, men who would have ended up in the system if not for Douglas and Patricia Boudreau. Instead of being hardened by life's hardships and bad circumstances beyond their control, they found a family who loved and accepted them, and gave them a place to call home. Sometimes brotherhood is more than sharing the same DNA.

This book is Heath Boudreau's story, and Heath was a hoot to write. He's a complicated man with a complicated history, but a loving heart. Though he's a complex man, Camilla is the perfect heroine for him. She's independent yet vulnerable, cares about her friends, but still carries some guilt about what her brother did to her best friend. A little gun shy, she loves fiercely and with her whole heart. I promise she's going to keep Heath on his toes.

If you've read my other romantic suspense books (the New Orleans Connection series and Cajun Connection series), you'll be familiar with the Boudreau name. Turns out there are a whole lot of Boudreaus out there, just itching to have their stories told. (Douglas is the brother of Gator Boudreau, patriarch of the New Orleans branch of the Boudreau family. Oh, and did I mention they have another brother – Hank "The Tank" Boudreau?)

So, sit back and relax. The pace of small-living might be less hectic than the big city, but small towns hold secrets, excitement, and heroes to ride to the rescue. And who doesn't love a Texas cowboy?

Kathy Ivan

EDITORIAL REVIEWS

"In Shiloh Springs, Kathy Ivan has crafted warm, engaging characters that will steal your heart and a mystery that will keep you reading to the very last page."

—Barb Han, *USA TODAY* and Publisher's Weekly
Bestselling Author

"Kathy Ivan's books are addictive, you can't read just one."

—Susan Stoker, NYT Bestselling Author

"Kathy Ivan's books give you everything you're looking for and so much more."

—Geri Foster, USA Today and NYT Bestselling Author of the
Falcon Securities Series

"This is the first I have read from Kathy Ivan and it won't be the last."

—Night Owl Reviews

"I highly recommend Desperate Choices. Readers can't go wrong here!"

—Melissa, Joyfully Reviewed

"I loved how the author wove a very intricate storyline with plenty of intriguing details that led to the final reveal…"

—Night Owl Reviews

Desperate Choices—Winner 2012 International Digital Award—Suspense

Desperate Choices—Best of Romance 2011 –Joyfully Reviewed

DEDICATIONS AND ACKNOWLEDGEMENTS

I love it when fans tell me they wish Shiloh Springs, Texas, was a real place, because they want to live there. Trust me, if it was real, I'd be your next door neighbor, because I want to live there too!

To the Readers! You are the reason I get up every day and head for the computer.

To my sister Mary. She knows why.

As always, I dedicate this and every book to my mother, Betty Sullivan. Her love of reading introduced me to books at a young age. I will always cherish the memories of talking books and romance.

More about Kathy and her books can be found at

WEBSITE:
www.kathyivan.com

Follow Kathy on Facebook at
facebook.com/kathyivanauthor

Follow Kathy on Twitter at
twitter.com/@kathyivan

Follow Kathy at BookBub
bookbub.com/profile/kathy-ivan

NEWSLETTER SIGN UP

Don't want to miss out on any new books, contests, and free stuff? Sign up to get my newsletter. I promise not to spam you, and only send out notifications/e-mails whenever there's a new release or contest/giveaway. Follow the link and join today!

http://eepurl.com/baqdRX

HEATH

CHAPTER ONE

Why won't they go away?

"Ms. Stewart? I need you to open your eyes now."

No. I want to sleep.

"No, no, Ms. Stewart. Come on, look at me. Let me see those pretty eyes, okay?"

Camilla didn't want to move. Everything hurt, even her eyelids. Noises assailed her from every direction, refusing to subside. It sounded like a hundred people crowded around her, all talking at once.

The woman's voice was insistent, and Camilla felt a hand gently shake her arm. It became obvious whoever wanted her awake wasn't about to give up or go away, which seemed wrong, because all Camilla wanted was to turn over and drift back to sleep.

A groan escaped her lips before she could bite it back. Shoot, now they knew she was playing possum. It took an extraordinary amount of effort to pry her eyelids open, and when she did, she wanted to slam them closed again.

Around her stood several people she didn't recognize, amidst overly bright lights and beeping sounds. A shout from the hallway had somebody in her little group scrambling toward the doorway. She could tell from the sound of squeaky shoes on the tiled floor moving farther away.

Great, she was in a hospital. From the assortment of beeps and hums, moans and groans of pain, her guess was the emergency room. She hated hospitals.

"Ms. Stewart...Camilla, I'm Dr. Forrest." A bright light shone in her eyes, first the right one and then the left, nearly blinding her. Blinking furiously, she struggled to sit up, but the burning pain in her arm froze her in place.

What the heck is wrong with me?

"What happened?" She muttered the words more to herself than anybody else, trying to figure out how she'd ended up in the hospital.

The sound of a masculine throat clearing shifted her focus from the doctor toward the tall, broad-shouldered man standing at the foot of her bed. The uniform and utility belt immediately gave him away as a cop. A tiny smile lifted the corners of his lips, and he gave a brief nod.

"Ms. Stewart, I'm Officer Dandridge. Glad to see you're awake. I need to ask you a few questions, if you're up for it. Can you tell me what you remember about the incident?"

Camilla's brow creased as she tried to piece things together, yet there was nothing but a big black hole of emptiness. She remembered her name, her parents, all the important pertinent details, but a chunk of her recent memories was gone.

"I don't remember what happened. How'd I end up in the hospital?"

Officer Dandridge pulled out a small notebook and jotted something down on the paper. His unreadable expression concerned her, because try as she might, she couldn't remember anything that'd happened. Had she been in a car accident? Fallen down the stairs in her townhouse and hit her head? Her heartbeat raced, because not knowing what happened scared her. Why couldn't she recall anything?

"Can you tell me the last thing you do remember?" He stood poised and composed, the tip of the pencil on the notepad, his expression veiled. He'd make a good cop on a TV show, she mused, because he didn't give anything away.

"I sorta remember having dinner with my parents. I didn't stay long because we got into an argument about Evan again. Evan's my brother." Her parents still refused to accept their son was a convicted felon who'd planned to kill his wife and sister-in-law over a ton of money he thought he could steal and get away with. Now he was sitting in a prison cell in Texas, and she'd been left to deal with the fallout.

Officer Dandridge glanced over at the doctor. "Has anybody notified her parents?"

"Let me check with intake. I know they contacted the person listed on her emergency contact information. I'll make sure to have her parents notified."

"Appreciate it." He smiled at Camilla. "When exactly was it you had dinner with your folks?"

"Sunday—no, Saturday night." Camilla lifted a hand to her forehead and winced. "Is anybody going to tell me what the heck happened to me? How'd I end up in the emergency room?"

Officer Dandridge glanced at her, concern on his face now instead of the expressionless mask he'd worn earlier. "You were found outside your townhouse. From witness statements, Ms. Stewart, you were the victim of an attempted carjacking."

Camilla shook her head before he'd even finished the sentence. "That's impossible. I don't own a car. I work from home, and pretty much everything I need is within walking distance."

"A neighbor reported finding you about twenty-five feet away from the gate to your townhouse. You've sustained an apparent gunshot wound. A bullet grazed your upper arm, close to the shoulder. We're not sure if a second bullet hit your forehead near the temple, or if you sustained that injury from the fall."

Camilla leaned back against the pillow, her mind reeling from the news. *Somebody shot me? I don't understand. Why would anybody want to hurt me?*

"Officer, we need to take Ms. Stewart for her CAT scan. If you need to ask her more questions, they'll have to wait." Dr. Forrest reached over and patted Camilla's forearm. "It's nothing to worry about, strictly routine in the case of head injuries with loss of consciousness. It won't hurt a bit, I promise."

"I understand, I guess. I wish I could remember what happened."

Dr. Forrest smiled sweetly, and typed information into her tablet before meeting Camilla's gaze. "It's not unusual to be unable to remember events surrounding a traumatic event, especially when you've sustained a head injury. You remember everything else, right? The only memories seem to be the short term ones, what happened around the time you got the lump on your head?"

Camilla nodded before deciding that wasn't a good idea, as a wave of vertigo caused her vision to blur. "That's right. I remember everything up to Saturday night. After that, there's nothing until I woke up here."

"It's called retrograde amnesia. It's probably nothing to worry about, but let's get you down for a CAT scan, and take a look, shall we? Then we'll know a little bit more about the situation, okay?"

"Sure."

Officer Dandridge handed Camilla a business card, and she clutched it in her hand, staring at him. She couldn't miss the compassion in his gaze. "Ms. Stewart, if you do remember anything, or have any questions, please don't hesitate to contact me. I've put your case number on the back of the card."

"Thank you."

As she watched him walk away, an orderly raised the side

rails on her bed, pushed it through the curtained-off cubicle, and into the hall. Her stomach clenched with every person they passed, her mind immediately questioning whether they'd been the one who attacked her. Television and movies always had the bad guy following the victim to the hospital to finish off their nefarious deeds.

Hands clenched into fists, she drew in a deep breath and then let it out slowly. After repeating the breathing exercise a couple of times, her body finally relaxed, and her heartbeat slowed to normal.

She hadn't lied to the nice policeman. While she couldn't remember who attacked her, there was one thing she did know. Something she hadn't told Officer Dandridge. While she didn't remember any of the details surrounding this latest attack, this wasn't the first time somebody tried to hurt her. She only wished she knew why.

Early the next morning, Heath Boudreau stormed through the electronic doors at the hospital main entrance, immediately zeroing in on the intake desk. His long strides ate up the distance, until he stood in front of the harried-looking girl, who couldn't be more than nineteen or twenty tops. Holding up his identification, he watched the overworked clerk glance his way, her fingers never stopping as she entered data into the computer system.

"I'm looking for Camilla Stewart. I understand she was admitted."

"Hang on a second, I'll be right with you."

He leaned in closer, not afraid to use his size to gain the answers he needed. Being several inches over six feet tall and built like a linebacker, he was used to people being intimidated by his size. The clerk barely glanced in his direction, her hands never leaving the keyboard.

"Ma'am, give me Ms. Stewart's room number, and I'll take it from there." The hardness in his voice had the clerk's head turning in his direction, and he watched her eyes widen at the ID he still held at her eye level, noting the ATF insignia and his name.

"Sorry, sir. Let me get that information right away." She typed in a few keystrokes, and he shoved his ID back into his pocket. "Ms. Stewart is in Room 615. Take the elevator to your right. When you get off, it'll be down the hall to your left."

"Thank you," he murmured before sprinting toward the elevator. The tightness in his gut hadn't alleviated. It had been a gigantic boulder from the minute he'd heard about Camilla being shot. He'd caught the red eye out of Dallas-Fort Worth, and he was sleepy, grumpy, and sadly lacking in caffeine. Didn't matter. All he cared about was getting to her, making sure she was alright. The sound of Beth's voice telling him Camilla had been shot still echoed in his head, repeating like a doomsday mantra over and over.

He mashed the elevator button again, knowing it wouldn't do a lick of good, but it made him feel better. When the doors whooshed open, he strode through, hitting the sixth-floor button. He didn't have a clue what he'd say to Camilla once he got there, but as long as she was okay, that was all that mattered.

He barely kept from racing down the hallway, looking for Room 615. Quietly pushing open the door, he let out the breath he hadn't known he'd been holding. Camilla lay against the sterile whiteness of the hospital pillows, her skin paler than he'd like. But she still looked beautiful.

Right off, he spotted the bandage on her forehead, its starkness blatantly incongruous against her creamy skin. She moaned softly in her sleep, and he moved farther into the room, reaching out and lightly touching her hand. She calmed instantly at his soft touch.

Closing his eyes, he whispered a brief prayer she was okay. He pulled the lone chair to the side of the bed, and slid onto it, wrapping her delicate hand in his. The flight had seemed to take forever, and he hadn't caught a wink of sleep, worrying about what he'd find when he got to the hospital.

He wasn't sure how long he sat there, holding onto her hand like a lifeline, before a nurse eased open the door. Straightening in the chair, wary and on guard, she smiled at him, and pointed toward the monitors hooked up to Camilla.

"I need to check her vitals. It won't take a second."

After she'd entered her data onto her tablet, she started for the door, and he quietly followed her out into the hall.

"How's she doing?"

"Ms. Stewart's going to be fine." She gave him a gentle smile. "The doctor gave her something for sleep, but she should be waking up soon."

"Can you tell me what happened to her?"

She shook her head. "Sorry, I just came on shift a little while ago. Are you a relative of Ms. Stewart's?"

"A friend."

"I'm afraid I can't really tell you anything without the patient's consent. HIPAA regulations don't allow it."

"I understand. Can you tell me if there's a specific police officer working her case, a name for me to contact?"

She typed on her tablet and scrolled through until she stopped. "Looks like Officer Dandridge is the lead investigator. You can reach him at this number." She rattled off a string of numbers, and Heath plugged them into his phone.

"Thanks."

"No problem. The doctor should be around to see her in the next hour or so." She gave him another half-hearted smile and left, headed for the next room down the hall.

Knowing hospitals frowned on the use of cell phones, he headed toward the elevator. He'd run downstairs, grab some coffee, and make a call to Officer Dandridge.

Once he'd paid for his coffee, he moved to one of the tiny bistro-type tables and wedged himself into the corner before taking a long drink of the black coffee. He hoped the caffeine would hit his system quickly, because he needed the jolt. With a grimace, he hit dial, and listened to the ringing.

"Dandridge."

Heath sat up straighter, on hearing the man's voice on the other end. Honestly, he'd been expecting to get the guy's voice mail.

"Officer Dandridge, I'm Heath Boudreau. I got your number from one of the nurses at the hospital. I'm calling regarding Camilla Stewart."

"Mr. Boudreau. Are you a relative of Ms. Stewart's?"

The man on the other end of the line sounded like a no-nonsense officer, so Heath got right to the point.

"No, I'm a friend. Her emergency contact, Beth Stewart, informed me Camilla had been shot. Since Beth knows I work for the ATF, she asked me to see what I could find out."

"Understood. Mr. Boudreau, there's not much I can tell you. I've talked with Ms. Stewart, although briefly, because the hospital needed to do some tests and perform a CAT scan. From what I've discerned thus far, through her statement and via witness accounts, Ms. Stewart was the apparent victim of a botched carjacking."

"Carjacking?" Heath hadn't expected that answer. But then, what had he expected?

"Ms. Stewart received a superficial GSW to her upper arm, which required stitches, as well as an injury to her forehead. I haven't heard back from the doctor as to whether the head injury was caused by a second bullet or as a result of her fall."

"Fall?" Heath was beginning to feel a bit like a parrot, repeating Officer Dandridge's words. "How'd she fall?"

"According to the witness, he stated when Ms. Stewart was hit in the arm or shoulder, she spun and tripped, hitting the asphalt in the parking area."

"Do you know if her car was stolen?"

"When I spoke with Ms. Stewart, she stated she didn't own a car."

Heath huffed out a breath, frustrated he wasn't getting a straight answer from the cop. "Then why are you saying it's an attempted carjacking? Since Camilla doesn't own one, the facts don't jibe."

"I agree, Mr. Boudreau. Like I said, I didn't get to talk with Ms. Stewart very long yesterday after they brought her in, because the doctor took her for a CAT scan to see if there was any concussion or other brain injury. Also, she was having some difficulty remembering the events surrounding the incident."

His gut tightened at those words. "She's got amnesia?"

"No...well, only for the time surrounding the incident. Doc called it retrograde amnesia. She can still remember everything like her parents and friends, where she lives, stuff like that. The only blank spot is from Saturday night until yesterday when she woke up in the emergency room."

"Any idea if it's a permanent thing or—"

"I'm sorry, Mr. Boudreau, but that's all the information I've got at this time. I'm going to head over to the hospital in a couple of hours and talk with Ms. Stewart again. Hopefully, she'll have remembered more about what happened."

"I'd appreciate you keeping me posted."

"Will do," Dandridge answered.

Heath disconnected the call and tossed his now empty cup into the trash. Glancing at the time, he figured he'd better head back upstairs to try and catch the doctor, and find out a professional opinion on Camilla.

Before he even opened the door to her hospital room, he heard voices, and one of them didn't sound too happy. Easing inside, he spotted a tall, older man with a white coat on and a stethoscope draped around his neck. In his hands, he held an electronic tablet. Heath had noted most of the nursing staff and physicians seemed to carry them around, constantly making entries and checking information. Another sign of the electronic age of medicine.

"I don't need to stay here. I need to go home."

The physician, or who Heath suspected was her doctor, gave a soft, frustrated-sounding sigh. "Ms. Stewart, I urge you to stay. There are a couple more tests I'd like to run. The CAT scan didn't show any trauma, but with your memory loss, I'd like to run an MRI, just to play it safe."

"It's not necessary. Other than my arm aching a bit, I don't think there's anything I can't do as an outpatient.

There are things I have to get done, and they're not getting finished with me lying in bed. I have a deadline looming over my head, and I can't afford to miss it."

Heath watched the back and forth between Camilla and the doc, and if he'd been a betting man, his money was on Camilla. The slight frown marring her otherwise pretty face reinforced the determination behind her words, and he doubted the good doctor would win this round.

"Excuse me, folks." Heath stepped further into the room, bringing Camilla's startled gaze to meet his. "Doc, does she need to stay? Will it hinder her recovery if she goes home today? If she needs somebody to watch over her, make sure she takes her meds, and doesn't black out in the shower, I'll stick around and babysit her."

"Heath Boudreau, I do not need a babysitter. I'm perfectly capable of taking care of myself."

"And you're doing a mighty fine job of that, Miss Camilla. I'm sure you intended to get yourself shot. Oh, and let's not forget the concussion." He barely hid his smirk when she flung herself against her pillows, until he noticed her wince of pain.

She turned her attention back to the doctor. "I promise I'll follow your instructions to the letter. I'll take any medication you prescribe, but I need to be home. Nothing personal, but I'm not fond of hospitals."

"Nobody is. You sure I can't convince you to stay one more day?" At Camilla's nod, he continued. "Alright, as long as Mr...Boudreau, was it...agrees to stay with you and keep an eye on you, I'll discharge you. But, if you feel the slightest headache or any dizziness, I'm gonna insist he bring you back to the emergency room immediately. Am I clear?"

"I understand, and I'll make sure she follows your instructions." Heath ignored Camilla's eye roll and shook the physician's hand.

"I'll have somebody get the discharge paperwork handled and leave prescriptions for an antibiotic and a pain reliever. We'll set up an appointment in a week to see you again in my office."

"Thank you, Dr. Bennett. I promise I'll follow your rules."

He gave her a friendly smile, an avuncular twinkle now lighting his eyes, and he patted Camilla's hand. "You'd better. I do not want to have to explain to your parents if anything happens to you on my watch."

With that, he left, leaving Heath standing inside the room, watching Camilla closely. He didn't like how pale she looked, and for a moment second-guessed his support for her going home. Maybe it was too soon.

"Don't even start with me, buster. I'm not staying in this hospital bed a second longer. All I need is to get home and get some work done."

"You're not working today. Today you're getting your antibiotic and pain pill, taking both, and going to bed. Tomorrow is soon enough to start working."

14

He slow blinked when she stuck her tongue out at him. Looks like Miss Priss had a little more backbone than he'd given her credit for.

As a nurse hustled through the doorway to help Camilla, Heath stepped outside, allowing her privacy to get changed and do whatever it was they did to get her ready for discharge. He wondered how long it would be before he and Camilla butted heads again. It was inevitable. Getting a rise out of Camilla, watching the fire in her eyes, and her indomitable spirit, flirting with her and watching her blush, was quickly becoming his new favorite pastime.

Things were about to get interesting at Casa de Camilla.

CHAPTER TWO

"**N**o."

"Yes." Heath folded his arms over his massive chest, a mulish expression on his face, and she barely refrained from sticking her tongue out at him.

Camilla rolled her eyes at Heath and shoved her bloody shirt into the plastic bag the nurse provided. Luckily, they'd offered her a scrub top to wear home, because she really dreaded putting the icky, blood-encrusted one back on.

"Look, I'm perfectly capable of getting home all by my-self. You don't need to stick around."

"Now who's being stubborn? I'm already here, with a perfectly good rental car. I'm going to drive you home."

She laid the bag on the end of the hospital bed, and turned to face Heath again, surprised he was here in North Carolina, and more specifically, in her hospital room. She'd been speechless when she'd opened her eyes earlier and found him sitting beside her bed. The gentleness of his smile almost undid her, because the whole time she'd been in Shiloh Springs visiting Beth, she'd never seen the softer, gentler side of the grumpy giant. Nope, he'd been a thorn in her backside from the moment they'd met. Something about him seemed larger than life, and he'd zeroed in on her with a torpedo focus and made her visit—interesting seemed such a tame word for the roller-coaster ride of emotions she'd experienced every time she came face to face with Heath Boudreau.

"Why are you here?"

"I told you, Beth's worried about you. Since she's your emergency contact, she got the call from the hospital you'd been shot." His gaze seemed to bore straight into her, examining every nook and cranny, and leaving her feeling like she didn't quite measure up. "By the way, why's Beth your emergency contact? She lives halfway across the country, yet your parents live here. Shouldn't they have been the first call?"

"None of your business, nosy." She winced when she reached for the bag on the bed, pulling at the stitches in her arm. Everything about the last couple of days was still a total blank, right up until she opened her eyes in the emergency room. Officer Dandridge had left a message he'd be stopping by her townhouse to ask more questions, since she was going home.

"Ms. Stewart, I've got your discharge instructions printed out, and here's your prescription for the antibiotics and a pain reliever." The nurse who'd loaned her the shirt handed her several printed pages and two prescriptions. Camilla liked the cheerful woman, whose gentle touch and pleasant demeanor made things a bit easier, especially since she hated being in the hospital.

"Thanks. When can I get out of here? I appreciate everything and everybody who's helped me, but I want to go home."

"Lucky for you, I've got a wheelchair right outside the door." She grinned toward Heath. "You want to do the honors?"

He chuckled while Camilla bit back a groan. *Great, I bet he's going to pretend to be Mario Andretti, and race through the halls at breakneck speed.*

The nurse wheeled the chair into the room, and Camilla eyed it warily. "Can't I walk? I didn't hurt my legs, they work fine."

"Sorry, hospital policy. We've gotta make sure you make it out the doors in one piece. After that, you're free and clear."

With a wary glance at Heath, she slid onto the seat of the wheelchair, and placed the plastic bag and all the papers in her lap. "Take me home, please."

"My pleasure, darlin'."

Taking a deep breath, Camilla waited for Heath to swerve recklessly down the hall. Instead, he treated her like delicate glass, moving slowly and carefully to the elevator, making sure they didn't bump anything along the way. They rode down in silence, while the nurse went over the discharge instructions once again. Get plenty of rest. Don't get the stitches wet. Take the antibiotic twice a day for a week, and don't miss any. Use the pain medication if she needed it. Blah, blah, blah.

Heath wheeled her to the sliding front doors of the hospital and came around to squat in front of her. "I'm going to get the car and pull it up outside. I'll only be a couple of minutes. Stay here."

She made a cross-my-heart motion, biting back the smile that threatened. There was such a serious expression on his face, like he was afraid if he left her alone even for a second, she'd bolt. Nope, she was anxious to get home and get into a hot bath, and maybe take one of the aforementioned pain pills.

"Camilla?"

Glancing up, she saw her neighbor, William Davis, standing in front of her, leaning on his cane. That was surprising. She'd met the older man when he'd moved into the townhouse next door to hers. They'd spoken a few times, their paths crossing when they checked the mai, stuff like that. He seemed like a pleasant enough man, though she imagined he was a bit of a recluse—like her.

"Mr. Davis, what a nice surprise."

"How are you doing, Camilla? I've been worried about you, with everything that happened. It was quite a bit of excitement. Did the doctors get you all fixed up?"

Camilla pointed to the bandage on her forehead. "Turns out I've got a hard head. Really, I'm fine. They're letting me go home."

"Wonderful." He shifted his weight, leaning heavily on his cane. Camilla couldn't remember a single time she'd seem him without it. She'd wondered more than once what happened to his leg but didn't feel right asking.

"They've assured me there's no serious injury."

"But you were shot! There was blood everywhere."

Camilla sat a little straighter in the wheelchair. Mr. Davis had been there. Had he seen everything that happened? Maybe he could give her some answers.

"Mr. Davis—"

"How many times must I tell you call me William, dear?" The heavy lines beside his eyes crinkled when he smiled, and she felt herself smiling, too.

"William, did you see what happened?"

"Oh, yes indeed. It was dreadful. I'd come outside to check on Oscar. I let him out to do his business, and he started barking like crazy. At first, I thought he was barking at you, dear. You'd stopped to pet him, and you waved at me and started back to your home. Then there was this bang, and you spun around and fell. Scared me half to death."

"You saw what happened?"

"Yes, I did. Though it all happened so fast. I scooped up Oscar and put him in the house, and then came and checked on you. You were unconscious, and there was so much blood." His voice dropped to a whisper. "I thought you were dead."

Camilla's thoughts whirled. If Mr. Davis had seen every-thing, maybe he could tell her who the shooter was. With her memory being wonky, maybe he could fill in the blanks.

"I'm sorry if it scared you. Can you tell me what you saw? I'm kind of...sketchy on the details."

Mr. Davis' brow furrowed, and he studied her face. "What do you mean?

Camilla blew out her breath, and ran her free hand through her hair, wondering where Heath was. Shouldn't he be back with the car by now?

"I've got a slight concussion, and I'm having a bit of a problem remembering exactly what happened."

"What—you can't remember anything?" His words were laced with shock.

She shook her head softly, because any sudden move-ment made the headache, currently a dull roar, come screeching to the forefront. "I've got something they're calling retrograde amnesia. I should get all my memories back eventually, but for now it's all a big blank."

"That must be awful, dear. I gave a full report to the police when they arrived. I was the only witness, and they grilled me for a long time." He grinned, his face lighting. "I felt like I was in one of those TV shows I watch, where the cops keep asking questions and jotting down notes in their notebooks. I wish I could have told them more, but I really didn't see much. I only heard the shot and saw you fall."

"Well, I appreciate you're telling them what you know. I

hope they catch whoever did this. It's frustrating not knowing."

"Don't you worry. I'm sure the police will catch the miscreant and lock him up for good." He patted her hand. "Well, I've got to run. Let me know if there's anything you need, dear."

Camilla watched him walk through the sliding doors, the electronic woosh echoing behind him. She'd have to make certain to have him over for coffee and try and get more details from him. But first, she needed to get home herself.

She didn't have to wait long before she saw a white SUV pull up under the covered area outside the front doors. Heath jogged around and opened the passenger side door and came back into the lobby.

"Ready to go?"

"Absolutely."

Camilla found herself quickly ensconced in the front seat; seat belt clicked into place. Heath's gentleness surprised her. For all his size, and he was mammoth, he was careful with her, treating her like spun glass. She couldn't help comparing this compassionate, sweet man with the one she'd met when she'd visited Beth. That Heath? He'd been the bane of her existence, leaving her ready to pull her hair out. Except in her dreams. Oh, those dreams had definitely leaned toward her naughty side, and he'd played a starring role in every one of them.

"Give me your address, and I'll plug it into the GPS."

She rattled it off, and within a minute they were headed toward her place. Leaning back against the headrest, she studied the man beside her. With his size, she wasn't surprised by the SUV, because she couldn't picture him being comfortable in a sedan. Over six five, and broad-shouldered, he probably intimidated a lot of people—but not her. Nope, she'd gone toe-to-toe with him back in Texas and hadn't backed down. If she was honest, she'd enjoyed their little battles, the playful give and take. That wasn't to say he didn't drive her crazy—he did—but he'd never crossed the line from being a prank-playing pest to anything intimidating or scary.

During that visit, she'd found herself listening for the sound of his Harley, admiring the way he controlled all that chrome and steel, taming the beast to his will. She'd almost succumbed and asked him for a ride, but chickened out in the end. She'd been too afraid he'd find out she'd never been on a bike before, and making a fool of herself in front of Heath wasn't gonna happen.

"If you don't mind, I need to make a quick stop by the pharmacy and pick up the prescriptions the hospital called in."

"I know, darlin'. That's not a problem. Which one do you want to stop at?"

Camilla straightened in the seat, shifting gingerly beneath the seatbelt. "There's one not far from the townhouse I've used in the past. Make a right at the next light, and it'll be down two blocks on your right."

Heath followed her directions and pulled into the parking lot. "Looks like there's a drive through pharmacy. Can you pick it up there or do you need to go inside?"

"Drive through works for me."

Within minutes, the prescriptions were filled, and they headed for her townhouse. Camilla closed her eyes, wishing she could remember the events of the previous couple of days. It seemed implausible—impossible—somebody intended to hurt her intentionally. Just her luck, she was probably in the wrong place at the wrong time and was a victim of circumstance. That had to be it.

"Beth was really scared when she got the phone call you were in the hospital."

Camilla rubbed her hand over her forehead. "She's been my emergency contact for years. I guess it never dawned on me to change it after she and my brother got divorced. I hate she had to hear about the accident that way."

"Accident?"

"It had to be, right? Nobody's out to hurt me, why would they be? I'm a writer; I make my living sitting at a desk in my house. Most people wouldn't know who I am if I passed them on the street. I haven't done anything to be on anybody's hit list. I wish I could remember exactly what happened though."

"What do you remember?" Heath's calm voice soothed the hint of anxiety lingering beneath the surface, and Camilla realized he was probably as tired as she was; he'd flown most of the night to get here.

"The police keep asking me that question, and I keep giving them the same answer. I remember going to my parents for dinner on Saturday night. I left as soon as I could, because my parents are…difficult."

"How so?"

Camilla shook her head, picturing the laughing and smiling Boudreau clan. "You need to understand, my parents are nothing like yours. Your family is close knit and loving. My parents aren't. Don't get me wrong, I'm sure they loved me and Evan, but they aren't demonstrative. They're set in their ways and refuse to accept the world and people outside their little circle change and grow. Good things and bad things happen, and they seem to be oblivious to what's right under their noses." She shrugged before continuing. "I remember getting into an argument about Evan. Of course, it's always about Evan. They still can't or won't accept he did the things he did to Beth and Tessa. He was going to *kill* them. Coldheartedly and without remorse, because he wanted money. Yet, they're blind to his flaws. Convinced he's been railroaded by the local yokels in some backwater Texas town, and he'll be released on appeal. Nothing I say or do can convince them he's guilty. To my parents, he's the perfect son and brother, and I'm the turncoat traitor who refuses to see what's right in front of me."

"I'm sorry, Camilla. I had no idea things were rough

between you and your family."

She crossed her arms across her middle, moving her arm gingerly to keep from aggravating the stitches. "It is what it is. They're never going to change, but they are my parents, and I love them despite their pigheadedness."

Heath's hand left the steering wheel and gently patted her hand. "Sometimes dealing with parents sucks. I'm sorry."

Camilla drew in a ragged breath. "I remember walking home from their place. It's about a half mile from their house to mine, and I needed some fresh air to cool off my temper, and think about what I needed to do the next morning. After that, it's all a blank. A big empty whole of nothing, until I woke up in the emergency room."

"Which leaves almost forty-eight hours you can't remember? How about, when we get back to your place, we take a look at your computer? See if we can piece together a bit of your missing time, how's that sound?"

She shot him a huge smile. "Sounds like a great idea. What are you waiting for, mister? Drive."

CHAPTER THREE

Heath pulled up and parked in front of Camilla's townhouse. It was two stories, an end unit, which meant nobody lived on one side. He liked that. It meant less noise and fewer nosy neighbors butting their noses into stuff that wasn't their business. One of the things he hated about living in a large city, everybody lived on top of each other and yet nobody knew their neighbor's name. Home in Shiloh Springs, he had room to spread out. He could breathe there. In Virginia, he lived in an apartment on the eighth floor, with people constantly around. The only good thing was it had an exceptional gym space, which saved him time and money.

"Thanks for the ride." Camilla unclipped the seatbelt and reached for the door handle with her left hand.

"Not a chance, sweetheart. You're not getting rid of me that easy. Sit tight." Heath slid from the driver's seat and bounded around the front of the SUV, opening Camilla's door. Reaching inside, he slid his arms around her, easing her from the passenger seat. He noted the wince she tried to hide and wished, not for the first time, he could take away all her pain. What he wouldn't give for five minutes in a room alone with whoever took a potshot at her…

"Gimme a second, and I'll grab your stuff." Reaching into the back, he got her purse and the plastic bag containing her bloodstained clothes, and moved around to her left side, not wanting to accidentally jar her injured arm.

"I need my purse to get my house key."

He handed the wine-colored shoulder bag to Camilla and studied his surroundings again. The townhouses themselves were high-end luxury, and he noted the CCTV cameras mounted in the parking area. Each townhouse had a couple of spaces in front, although his rental now took up one of the spaces in front of Camilla's place. The other sat empty. He didn't like how the complex was encircled by a forested area. While it might be pretty and give the pretense of not being in the middle of the city, it was also extremely easy for somebody to hide in plain sight.

Each townhouse had a length of decorative wrought iron fencing about four feet high across the front and sides, parceling off separate front yard spaces for each individual unit. Camilla's was a bit larger than the rest, wrapped around the side of the building since she had an end unit. He made a mental note to get a look at the back of her townhouse and determine how easily somebody might sneak in without being caught on the CCTV cameras.

"Heath, I swear I'm fine. You don't have to see me into my house. I'm perfectly capable of unlocking a door."

"I'm sure you are, sugar, but I'd rather you be safe than sorry. Let me take a look around, so I can tell Beth everything's okay, and get you settled. You can grouse all you want, but you're not getting rid of me until I'm satisfied. Hand over the keys, and let's get you inside."

He didn't bother adding he didn't like the fact she was standing out in the open, pretty much in the same spot where she'd been shot. After spotting those cameras, he knew he'd be making another call to Officer Dandridge. Getting a look at the CCTV footage moved up on his list of things to check out.

Opening the front door, he moved in first, his eyes scanning every inch. There was a small entryway that opened up into an open floor plan, making the living space one large area. Good, not a lot of places to hide when everything was in plain view.

"Can I come in now, or do you want me to keep standing on the front porch?"

Instead of answering, he reached back and grabbed her left hand, and tugged her through the doorway. The disgruntled look she shot him amused him. When she tugged on her hand, he held tight, towing her in his wake as he headed toward the kitchen. Pointing to one of the bar stools lined like soldiers in front of the huge kitchen island, he raised a brow and waited, wondering if she'd follow his lead, or give him a hard time. He suspected the latter.

"Wait here while I check the rest of the place. I'll get

your pain medication when I come back."

She stood beside the island, her foot tapping on the hardwood floor. Tap, tap, tap. *Uh, oh.*

"Seriously? Not a chance. I either go with you or I follow you."

Throwing his hands up, he spun around and headed down the hall, hearing the light clicking of her heels as she followed behind. He grinned, knowing she couldn't see it. Everything about her spoke to him on some deep level. Though she was a city gal, she reminded him of his momma.

He held up his hand when he came to the first closed door.

"My office," she whispered from behind him.

He silently turned the knob and eased the door open, not sure what he expected to happen. It wasn't likely anybody lurked around every corner, waiting to attack Camilla the minute she came within reach. Still, he wasn't about to take any chances. More than likely, the incident was a botched robbery, though he really wanted to speak to the witness who'd talked with Dandridge.

Walking further into the room, he studied her work-space, noting she had a pretty decent setup. Her desk was set up facing the door, with a window behind her. A desktop computer with one of the biggest monitors he'd ever seen took up most of the space, along with an ergonomic keyboard and mouse. A printer sat on a stand in the corner, and a tall, tree-like plant sat in the other corner, nearest the window.

"Nice plant."

"Thanks."

He walked over to the closet and pulled the double doors open, finding the inside lined with shelves, crammed full of notebooks, folders, pens, and more journals than he'd ever seen outside an office supply store. He chuckled at the sight, because everything was an explosion of pink. Pink pens, pink notebooks, bejeweled everything. Even the sticky notes were pink in every shade imaginable.

"Not a word, tough guy."

"But everything's so pink and sparkly."

"I'm a girl. We like pink and sparkly." He took note of how she bit her lip to keep from laughing, her eyes filled with mirth.

"I had noticed." He watched the wash of color spill across her cheeks, eyes downcast. "Let's check the other rooms, and get you settled."

Without another word, he walked down the hall to the other partially closed door. He drew in a deep breath and stopped in his tracks, because it smelled like Camilla. The scent was familiar, a soft floral with hints of roses. He'd memorized that scent when she'd been visiting Shiloh Springs, and it had haunted him. Every time he'd walked past anything rose scented, he immediately thought of her.

"Heath?"

Closing his eyes for the briefest second, he braced himself

and flung open the door, stepping inside quickly. On first perusal, nothing looked out of place. A large, queen-sized bed dominated the far wall, a large headboard and footboard anchoring it in place. Directly across stood a set of French doors leading out to a deck covered with an open pergola. He refused to get drawn into admiring the room, focused instead of finding any hint of danger.

Striding across the room, he spotted two doors, and grabbed the handle of the first one, pulling it open. An enormous walk-in closet dominated the area, filled with open shelves, and the big closet organizer with drawers and baskets. One entire section was filled with nothing but shoes and handbags.

Wordlessly, he turned and stared at Camilla, who shrugged. He could almost hear her repeating "I'm a girl", like she had in the office. Recognizing nobody could possibly be hiding in there, he walked out and opened the only other door in the room.

An elegantly appointed bathroom was behind this one. Double sinks and a massive shower filled the space. A jetted tub sat beneath a window. While it was nice, he wasn't overwhelmed. As long as there was a toilet and a shower, that pretty much filled his needs.

"Um, Heath?"

He looked back at Camilla, whose face appeared decidedly paler than it had been a few minutes ago.

"What's wrong?"

With a shaky hand, she pointed to the partially-made bed, and drew in a deep breath. "That's not the way I left it. I make my bed every morning. Somebody's been here."

Camilla stared at the crumpled bedspread, partially pulled from beneath the stack of decorative pillows. She knew she'd made the bed Saturday morning. It was part of her daily ritual. Besides, the throw pillows would've been stacked by the nightstand if she hadn't. Instead, they were atop the mattress, but the oversized purple and silver-toned quilt she used was wadded up beneath the pillows, like it had been hastily pushed back into place.

"Are you sure?"

She nodded. "Positive. I can be a bit OCD about routine. I know I made the bed. Now," she gestured toward the disturbed cover, "that's definitely not how I'd do it."

Heath put his hands atop her shoulders, careful not to touch the bandage on her arm, and stared down into her eyes, his gaze revealing nothing. Yet her legs felt like jelly, and her stomach did that little flip-floppy thing it did every time she saw him.

"I want you to go into the living room, right now. No questions. Go."

"What? No, I—"

"Please, Camilla, you need to get out of here."

Hands on her hips, she knew if she didn't stand her ground, he'd treat her like a fragile porcelain doll and wrap her in bubble wrap, and she wasn't having it. She'd worked for too long and too hard to become a strong, independent woman, breaking free of the cultural mores of her family, to take a step back now.

"I'm staying. Besides, there's nobody here."

Heath sighed. "Wrong. There's somebody here—or rather something. Listen."

Camilla stood silently, straining to hear whatever it was Heath meant. Finally, there was the slightest sound of…a rattle? It was faint, like the sound was muffled, but it wasn't random, instead a steady sound and it was coming from her bed.

"Camilla?"

"Yeah?"

"If you're staying, do me a favor and open those French doors, then stand out of the way, okay?"

Sprinting across the room, she unlocked the deadbolt and flung the doors wide, feeling the breeze brush against her skin. One of the doors hit the wall and started swinging closed again, and she caught it, easing it back open. Turning around, she noted Heath had moved closer to her bed, his eyes glued to the bedspread.

Heart in her throat, she edged her way across the room, toward the bedroom door, and watched his every move. She barely breathed; her body frozen in fear. Her brain told her what was under the covers, but subconsciously she didn't want to believe it. It was impossible.

Almost faster than her eyes could track, Heath leapt toward her bed, scooping the bedding into his arms in a jumbled bundle, and raced toward the back patio, and tossed it as far as he could. After the throw, he took a couple of steps back, and slammed the French doors closed. She heard the heavy breath soughing in and out of his mouth as he bent forward, hands on his knees.

Moving to stand beside him, she watched the pile of material in the middle of her back deck, anticipation rocketing through her blood. Long moments passed and she started thinking maybe they'd made a mistake. After all, what were the chances something ended up in her bed?

Before she could finish her thought, the edge of the bed-spread shifted the smallest amount, and her breath caught in her lungs. Aw, shoot, he'd been right. The sounds of rattling grew louder, through the open door, and Camilla's eyes widened as a triangular-shaped head emerged from beneath the cloth.

"Step back." Heath stared out the French doors, eyes glued to the back patio. Camilla moved forward a couple paces and pressed her hand against the glass. The sinewy body emerged completely from beneath her bedspread, undulating in an almost hypnotic dance, the end of its tail quivering feverishly.

"Pack a bag." Heath grabbed his cell phone from his

pocket, as he strode toward the living room.

"Wait, hang on a second. What do you mean, pack a bag?" She raced to catch up to him and watched him turn toward the kitchen. "I'm not going anywhere."

Ignoring her, he spoke quietly into his phone. She watched him, taking in the strong jawline, the sharp angle of his cheekbones, and his deep sapphire blue eyes. He ran a hand through his dark blond hair, and it fell into mussed waves. It was a habit she'd noted when she'd been in Shiloh Springs.

"That's right. You might want to contact animal control or somebody and let them know to check around the building. Yeah, it was definitely a rattler, maybe three feet long. Nope, sorry, didn't have time to capture it, I was too busy getting it out of Ms. Stewart's bed. You heard me, it was in her bed, under the blankets."

A frown crossed his face as he listened to whoever was on the other end of the phone. At one point, he did an eye roll that had the corners of her lips turning up.

"Listen, I might chalk it up to a fluke if it was simply one incident. But first somebody took a shot at her, and now there's a venomous snake inside her locked townhouse. That's one time too many."

He paced as he spoke, his large body seeming to take up all the space in her kitchen. Whatever the person on the other end of the phone said, Heath wasn't buying it.

"Absolutely. I think it's probably the best course of action at this point. We'll be leaving ASAP. No, I'm not going to say where we'll be, but I'll stay in touch. We'll be gone a couple of days, maybe longer," she heard Heath say, and he pinched the bridge of his nose, and listened to whoever was on the other end. "Yeah, it's a family thing. Thanks. I'll be in touch."

Camilla moved across the kitchen to the island, where Heath had left the bag containing her clothes and her meds. It was time for her antibiotic, and it might be a good idea to take one of the pain pills, too. She crossed to the sink and poured a glass of water and sat it beside the pill bottles.

Heath hung up the phone and turned to meet her gaze. "Why aren't you packing?"

"Because I'm not going anywhere. Who were you talking with?"

"Officer Dandridge, giving him the lowdown on what happened. Listen, darlin', we both agree you can't stay here. It's not safe."

"Heath, I'm a big girl. I can take care of myself."

"Tell me, Camilla, what would you have done if I hadn't been here? Hadn't realized somebody had been in your home until it was too late?"

She didn't want to admit he was right, even if he was. Chances were good she'd have headed for her room and flopped down on the bed, without giving it more than a cursory glance. No chance she wouldn't have been bitten who knows how many times.

"You're right. It's just...I can't...it's all too much. I don't understand why any of this is happening."

He walked over and placed his hand beneath her chin, tilting her head up. "One incident I might chalk up to an accident, a botched snatch and grab robbery. But can you really say a rattlesnake in your bed, *in your bed*, is a coincidence?"

"Gah! I can't remember anything. Heath, this doesn't make any sense. Who'd do this?"

Heath pulled her close in a gentle hug. She rested her head against his chest and wrapped one arm around his waist. It was so nice to be in his arms, to feel comforted and safe, even if for only a moment. A hand ran softly up and down her spine, and she sighed, hoping the moment would last. Of course, that didn't happen, because Heath opened his mouth again and the spell was broken.

"I want to take you to the ranch. You should be safe there. At least with Momma and Dad around, you can't get into too much trouble."

She thumped him in the stomach with the back of her hand, and he turned her loose. Taking a step back, she glared at him. "This is not my fault. I am not going to run away and hide at your family's ranch. They barely know me! I will not be bringing my trouble to their doorstep, and you can't make me."

His eyes narrowed, and she knew he was fighting the urge to toss her over his shoulder and carry her from the townhouse. Typical caveman mentality. Man save woman. Grunt, grunt. Probably the only thing keeping him from acting on his instincts was the fact she'd been shot the day before. Not what she'd consider a lucky break, but it kept her standing on her own two feet.

"Cam…"

"Cam? Since when do you call me Cam?"

His little boy grin was infectious, and she found herself responding. "What? I think it's cute."

"Nobody calls me that."

"Good. I like being the only one to call you Cam."

She felt heat washing her cheeks, and knew she needed a distraction, pronto. Fumbling with the pill bottle, she poured one of the antibiotic pills from the container into the palm of her hand. She picked up the bottle with the pain pills, held it for a couple of seconds, and then plunked it back onto the countertop. With her luck, it would knock her out for hours, and he'd simply put her in the car and start driving. Couldn't have that happening. She had deadlines looming, and unfortunately, wasn't even close to finishing unless she put in about a week's worth of all-nighters.

"I'm sorry, darlin', I forgot you just got out of the hospital. Why don't you take your meds, and yes, the pain pill too, and I'll go and make up your bed? You can get some rest, and we'll talk about everything when you wake up. A couple of hours won't make much of a difference."

When her jaw cracked at her yawn, she realized he was

right, and she needed to get some sleep. She'd barely slept a wink in the hospital, between the noise, people coming in and out of her room half the night, and her head and arm hurting. Maybe she'd be thinking clearer if she did get some rest.

"Okay. The TV remote is on the coffee table, and there's plenty of food in the fridge. Snacks in the pantry." She pointed to the door off to the right. "Heath...thanks for coming."

"I'll always be here for you, sweetheart." He brushed a kiss against her forehead, right beside the bandage. "Now, where do you keep the extra blankets, because I'm not going outside to get the other one until I'm sure our slithery friend is long gone."

"Top shelf in the hall closet."

With a wink he strode away, and she bit back a sigh. She couldn't let foolish dreams of a future with this particular Boudreau take shape, because he'd be gone soon, and she refused to be one of those women who bemoaned what might have been.

She got the pain pill out of the bottle, and gulped it down with the water, and closed her eyes for a moment, before straightening her spine and mustering her determination, a plan already forming in the back of her mind.

Nobody was going to get the best of her. Not now. Not ever.

CHAPTER FOUR

Heath waited until he was sure Camilla was asleep before pulling his phone from his pocket and dialing. He heard the ringing, although only halfway paying attention. Instead, the events from earlier played over and over in his mind, a whole list of "what ifs" leaving him with a sick feeling in the pit of his stomach.

"Hello?"

"Uncle Gator, it's Heath."

"Well, well, I haven't heard from you in forever, boy. You doing okay?"

"I'm good, but I've got a friend who's having a bit of a problem. Hoping you might give me a hand. She's attracted some unwanted attention that's escalated into violence, and I think she needs to get out of town for a bit."

Though it had been ages since he'd seen his uncle face-to-face, he could picture the scowl on his uncle's face at his words. Etienne "Gator" Boudreau was his dad's big brother, and he'd been raised with the same morals and values Douglas Boudreau had, ones he'd instilled in all his children. Gator's sons were all ex-military men, working for one of the premiere security services in the country, run by a man named Samuel Carpenter. Carpenter was a billionaire, with more money than he'd ever spend in several lifetimes, and hired the best. Being part of the Boudreau clan, Heath had met the man several times. Though he wouldn't say they were bosom buds, he trusted Carpenter and the men who worked for him.

"What kind of trouble are we talking about, son?"

"I'm not sure on all the details yet. Police are investigating, though they haven't come up with anything. Cam was shot in front of her townhome and ended up in the emergency room with an upper arm injury and a laceration to her head. The injury isn't serious, more a furrow where the bullet raked a furrow across the skin. The doctor isn't sure if the head injury came from a bullet graze or from a fall. Apparently, she hit the parking lot pavement after the shooting started. So, it's unclear whether one or two shots were fired."

Gator whistled. "What'd she do to have somebody taking potshots at her?"

Heath sighed and raked a hand through his hair, feeling the frustration eating at him. "That's part of the problem. She doesn't remember. The emergency room doctor said she's got something called retrograde amnesia. They did a CAT scan, and it didn't show any damage. Short story, she can remember everything up through Saturday night. Everything after that until the time she woke in the hospital is gone."

"Huh. Makes it kinda hard to figure out who wants to hurt your gal if she can't remember why somebody would be after her in the first place."

His gal. Heath flung himself onto the sofa and ran his free hand over his forehead. He had the beginning of a headache and wondered if Camilla had any aspirin. Not that he was about to wake her up to find out. He'd explore the bathroom cabinet after he hung up.

Gator wasn't telling him anything he hadn't already figured out, and it was driving him crazy. Finding out who wanted to hurt Camilla topped his list of priorities. Once he hung up from talking with Gator, he'd need to call Officer Dandridge again, and let the cop know his plans for Camilla.

"That's not the only thing that's happened, Uncle. I brought her home from the hospital a couple hours ago, thinking to get her settled and do a bit of subtle questioning. Never got the chance. Found a rattlesnake curled up underneath the covers on her bed."

Gator whistled long and low. "Not something she'd see every day unless she lived out in the country. But you mentioned a townhouse, so I'm guessing no."

"Cam's definitely a city girl." Heath smiled, remembering how much fun he'd had teasing her when she visited the family's ranch. "One incident I can buy as an accident. Police are investigating the shooting as a botched carjacking, though they now know Cam doesn't own a car. I've been talking to the local cop in charge, name's Dandridge. Seems to have a decent head on his shoulders, and he's not taking anything at face value."

There was a long pause, and Heath pondered what Gator thought, because he knew his uncle had a mind like a steel trap. Known as Mr. Fix-It throughout the environs of New Orleans, he was the go-to guy when you had a problem. Big or small, if Gator considered your situation needed the kind of attention that skirted outside the boundaries of what was deemed socially or legally acceptable, he'd find a way to ameliorate the issue. The stakes increased tenfold if it seemed like there was a damsel in distress. Gator had been known to play the White Knight a time or two.

"Seems to me you might want to consider taking your gal out of town for a while, at least until the authorities can determine who's after her." There was the slightest pause before the word authorities, which sent a chill skittering along Heath's spine, because he had the feeling his Uncle Gator had decided to take an up close and personal look into Camilla's case.

"That's why I called you. Whether she likes it or not, Cam's leaving. I do expect her to put up a fuss, but I think I can convince her to head to the ranch. She's got family there, but I want to make a couple of detours along the way. Don't want to take a straight flight, too easy to track. Wondered if we might stay with you for a day or two?"

"I don't think your gal would be comfortable at our

cabin in the bayou, probably a little too back to nature for a city gal. Ranger and Sarah are out of town for a couple of weeks, visiting her folks in San Diego. Bet Ranger wouldn't mind you using the apartment. Since they bought the bigger house, they're rarely there anyway."

Heath felt his muscles relax with his uncle's suggestion. He hadn't realized how tense he'd gotten. Guess the situation with the rattler and the knowledge somebody was after Camilla hit a little closer to home than he cared to admit.

"Thanks, Uncle Gator. That takes a weight off my shoulders. I'm going to try and arrange a flight from North Carolina to New Orleans—"

"Stop. If you think somebody's gonna be checking the airlines, and nowadays anybody can who's a halfway decent computer user, you don't want to go that route. I doubt you've had time to get acceptable fake ID, so let me handle transportation. Samuel won't have a problem with me borrowing the company jet. Gimme a couple of hours, and I'll get back to you with the details."

"If you're sure he won't mind, that's actually a great idea. I bet Cam will get a kick out of me having access to a million-dollar private jet," Heath chuckled, imagining the expression on her face. This might actually be fun. Ideas were already spinning of ways to tease and torment her.

"Talk to you soon."

Gator was gone before Heath even said goodbye.

One more phone call to Dandridge, because he wanted the cop to know he was taking Camilla out of the line of fire, though he wasn't about to tell him where they were headed. That was on a strict need-to-know basis, and right now Officer Dandridge didn't qualify for that category.

Next came the hard part. Convincing Camilla to head to Texas—via New Orleans.

CHAPTER FIVE

"**R**eady to finish our conversation? The one about hitting the road? I'd love to take you for a ride." He waggled his brows suggestively, and she blew him a raspberry. After having spent a mostly sleepless night in the hospital, and now taking a pain pill-induced nap, Camilla had woken up starving and in need of a long, hot shower. She'd grabbed the list of takeout menus from her kitchen drawer, told him to pick something, and headed for the bathroom.

One look at her face, and she'd swallowed hard. The skin over the right side of her forehead was covered with a bandage, where the cut above her eye had bled profusely. She swallowed again, remembering waking up in the emergency room and seeing all her blood-soaked clothing, along with the stacks of gauze they'd used to clean her up while she'd been unconscious. But worse, her right eye was puffy and swollen, discolored with dark bruises, ringing the outside so she resembled a one-eyed raccoon.

"Guess it could be worse. I could have lost it." Reaching up, she gingerly touched the discoloration. While it hurt, it was bearable. Turning on the shower, she cranked the temperature up to hot, and let the water run while she pulled off the clothes she'd fallen asleep in. The pain pill must've had a surprisingly good kick, because she never slept in her clothes.

She showered and washed her hair, being careful to keep the bandage as dry as possible, quite a trick with the limited use she had with her injured arm. The doctor's instructions said she could leave off the sling if she didn't need it, and she'd tossed it on the pile of clothes on the floor. While movement of the arm wasn't comfortable, it wasn't unbearable, at least with the lingering effects of the pain med still in her system. She'd use it later, if she needed it.

She finally climbed out of the shower when the water turned cold, and she felt clean. Picking up the loose-fitting pajamas and robe she'd brought into the bathroom, she quickly dressed, and wandered into the kitchen.

"Hope Chinese is okay."

"I love it."

"Good, it should be here soon. In the meantime, we need to talk." Heath patted a stool next to him at the extended counter, and Camilla sighed. Might as well get this conversation over with, because after she ate, she needed to get some work done. Her book wasn't going to write itself.

"Heath—"

"I know you're thinking you can stay here, you don't believe somebody's targeted you. Maybe you're right, and these incidences are simply random acts that weren't intended for you. But I want you to think carefully about what I'm saying before you answer. What if they aren't coincidences?" He held up his hand when she started to interrupt, cutting off her objection. "I said think about what you can remember. Think about what's happened since you woke up in the hospital. Look at each incident like they'd happened to somebody else. What if it were Beth who'd been shot at? Or Beth who came home to find a venomous snake in her bed? What would you tell her to do? Be honest, Cam. What's your gut telling you?"

She huffed out a loud sigh, because if it had been Beth, or Tessa, or any one of her friends, her gut instinct would have screamed for them to hightail it out of town, and let the cops figure out who the villain was. Toss them in jail, heck, under the jail, never to see the light of day again.

The corners of Heath's lips tipped upward, though his eyes remained serious. "I've made arrangements for us to head to Texas. We've got time for an early supper and then we'll head to the airport."

"What? Heath, I can't up and leave just like that. I need to pack. I...I have a deadline I can't miss. Besides, there's no way you could have gotten plane tickets out tonight without paying a fortune."

"Don't worry about the transportation, it's all been handled. The plane will be ready and waiting at the airport whenever we're ready."

Her eyes widened with every word. "Waiting at the airport? Who are you, Mr. Moneybags?"

"Let's just say I've got friends in high places."

The doorbell rang before she could shoot back a scathing retort. When she started to get up, Heath shot her a look which froze her in her seat, lifting her hands in surrender. Without a word, he headed for the front door, checking to see who was outside before answering. She heard the murmur of voices, and the closing of the front door, but since her back was to the front area, she couldn't see who was there. A few seconds later, the delicious scent of food hit her, and her stomach rumbled.

Setting the bags down on the counter, Heath opened cabinets until he found plates and glasses. He easily found the silverware and set it alongside the plates.

"This conversation isn't over, but you need to eat."

"Pass me the sweet and sour chicken."

Heath handed her the container and pulled out the rest, laying them on the countertop between their plates. He then filled their glasses with water and ice, and sat down beside her. It wasn't the fact he was seated too close that had her heartbeat racing, she chided herself. Nope, wasn't the fact he smelled even better than the buffet laid before her. Staring at her loaded plate, she stabbed a piece of chicken and dipped it into the sauce, shoving it into her mouth before she said something she shouldn't. Like how much she'd missed him. Or that she secretly enjoyed their banter, and the way he refused to curse, no matter how much he was provoked.

That fact tickled her more than she wanted to admit. This big, fierce-looking man, who worked a job where he faced danger on a daily basis, wouldn't cuss. There had to be a story there, and she'd wheedle it out of him eventually.

They ate in relative silence, and her brain raced, trying to come up with a reasonable and logical excuse to stay home. A losing battle, to be sure, but at least she had to try.

"Stop overthinking things, sweetheart. I've already notified Dandridge you're going out of town for a little while. Didn't tell him where, because the fewer people who know, the better."

"Heath, I really can't up and leave."

"Beth told me you could work anywhere there was a Wi-Fi connection and a computer. Was she wrong?"

Camilla nibbled on her lower lip, considering her answer. "Yes and no. If I have my laptop, I can probably make it work. I need a really reliable Wi-Fi connection. I have to be online every day. Social media, e-mail, and a whole host of other stuff. I might be able to miss a day, two at the most, but most of my livelihood depends on my keeping in touch with my readers."

"Readers?" Heath grinned. "Do you know, I think that's the first time I've ever heard what you do. What do you write? Anything I might have read?"

Heat spread across her cheeks in a rush. She wasn't ashamed of what she wrote. Hardly. She was darned proud she wrote books fans clamored for, urging her to write more and faster. Sometimes, though, people didn't understand the appeal of writing or reading romance, especially men.

"I doubt you've read my books, and I write under a pen name."

Heath rested his chin on his fist and studied her with an intensity that had her fighting to keep from squirming in her seat. "Now you've got me curious."

With deliberate ease, she set her fork on her plate before answering. "I write romance. Specifically, romantic suspense books. And, yes, before you ask, there is sex in them. Hot, steamy, sweaty sex."

Heath straightened. "Why would you think I'd think there's something wrong with writing something you obviously love?"

Camilla shook her head. "Sorry, it's kind of a knee jerk reaction now. Most men, present company excluded," she added with a tentative smile, "automatically think all romance books are bodice-rippers or smutty, dirty, soft porn for housewives. It infuriates me, to tell you the truth, but I'm too tired of defending myself to them. So I usually don't mention what I write."

"I think it's amazing you can write. I know it's hard work. Look, my brother is an investigative reporter. I see how hard he works, and that's with writing a few thousand words. You're writing tens of thousands of words and telling complete stories. I'd never look down on that or consider it frivolous. No matter the subject matter, it's bloody hard work, and I'm impressed."

"Thanks. You're in the minority. Of course, most of the time I can ignore it because the naysayers are mostly uninformed or haven't read a book since they got out of school. I'm pretty thick skinned. As they say in my business, I laugh all the way to the bank."

When Heath chuckled, she knew he really got it. Wouldn't it be nice to be able to be herself around him? Would he understand how important her writing was? For her, writing felt as integral as breathing. Thinking about not being able to put new words on the page every day? Inconceivable.

He leaned against the stool's back, his posture calm and relaxed. "Tell me about your books. You mentioned a pen name?"

"My agent and I decided it would be a good idea, since I'm single and live alone, to use a pen name. I also have my own publishing company imprint, as further protection."

"Smart. How long have you been writing?"

"I've been writing on and off my whole life, but I started writing seriously about eight years ago. I signed my first publishing contract seven years ago. I'm what people in the industry call a hybrid author. I have traditionally published books by large publishers, and I also independently publish others."

"Wow, the more I hear, the more I'm impressed with what you've accomplished. And in case you're wondering, I would never look down on anybody for writing romance. I know better. Don't forget, I have a sister and a mother, and they both read them."

"Really? I guess we never talked about it while I was visiting Beth."

Heath chuckled, the sound sliding against Camilla's skin and making her shiver. "There were times when I never saw Nica without her nose in a book. Even with all her classes at college, she still finds times for her precious books."

"That's nice to hear."

Standing, she started gathering the empty containers, napkins, and empty bag, tossing them into the trash. It frustrated her everything took so long, because of the stupid sling she'd ended up putting back on. Carrying the plates to the sink, she jumped when Heath's hands landed gently on her waist, turning her to face him.

"You know, as nice as this is, you're still not getting out of leaving with me tonight. I already packed a bag for you while you slept. Enough for a few days. We can pick up anything else you might need once we get to Shiloh Springs."

"Wait, what?" She sputtered out the protest. "You packed my clothes?" Her mind went blank for a second, before she pictured Heath rummaging through her dresser, and once again felt the blush heating her cheeks. "I…you…I can't believe you went through my things."

A smug smile curved his lips, and she almost wished she could wilt into a puddle on the floor. Heath now knew her secret obsession. The one not even her bestie, Beth, knew about. The one vice she indulged, ever since she'd started making enough money to afford it.

Sexy lingerie. Exclusive and selective—and, yes—expensive brands, with lots of silks and satins and lace. Skimpy, provocative, and luxurious to touch. High-end bras and panties, corsets, and the occasional bustier that made her feel feminine, attractive, and sensual. Alluring. It didn't matter that nobody saw them except her; it was her private indulgence. And now Heath knew her secret fantasy.

"I promise I didn't snoop." He held his hand across his heart, but the barely suppressed mirth shone in his eyes. "You have exquisite taste, Cam. If I ask nicely, will you model some of your ensembles for me?"

"Not in this lifetime, Cowboy."

"Seriously, sweetheart, all kidding aside, you need to grab anything you can't live without for the next several days, maybe a week, and toss it in the suitcase. I didn't touch your makeup or other stuff in your bathroom. I know how particular women are about that. I'll load up your laptop—"

"Let me do that. I know what I have to take, the stuff that's important. I need to get my thumb drive backups, although I also have everything backed up on the cloud. Need my password book, phone charger, laptop charger, and…"

"Less talking, more walking. We need to leave in half an hour."

Camilla shook her head and glared at Heath. "You're crazy. I'm crazy, too, because I'm listening to you. I still think you're overreacting, but, what the heck. Spending a few days with Beth and Jamie sounds nice."

She headed for her office. When she'd bought the townhouse, she'd converted a spare bedroom into a workspace where she felt comfortable doing her writing. Normally she wrote on a desktop computer, but kept everything updated on the laptop, in case she wanted to get out, and spend a couple of hours in a coffee shop, soaking up the atmosphere and binging on delightfully flavored caffeine.

Snatching up her computer bag, she shoved her laptop inside, along with the charger. Next went in her thumb drives, which she had hooked onto a keyring, easier to keep them all together. Her list of passwords was tossed into the outside pocket. Glancing around, she impulsively decided to toss in a couple of paperbacks of her latest release. If Nica was a big reader, maybe she'd like a copy.

She left the laptop case leaning against the wall outside the office, and walked into her bedroom, and headed straight to the master bathroom. Moving carefully, she grabbed her makeup bag, toothpaste and toothbrush, and finally her hairbrush. She carried them into the bedroom and tossed everything onto the bed, wincing when she felt the muscles in her arm pull. Opening the closet door, she pulled a peasant top and long crinkled skirt off hangers and picked up a pair of black ballet flats. If she was going to be flying, she was going to be comfortable. Well, as comfortable as she could be with two gunshot wounds.

Dressing quickly, she turned and jumped, clutching at her chest, seeing Heath standing in the open doorway.

"You ready?"

"I need to get the suitcase out of the closet and add my toiletries. Otherwise, I'm good to go."

Without a word, he walked through the open closet door, and lifted the suitcase free, laying it on the bed. With a motion almost faster than she could follow, he flipped open the suitcase's lid, tossed everything inside, and closed it, lickety-split.

"I took the trash out to the dumpster, so the place doesn't stink when you come back. We really need to get to the airport." He grabbed her suitcase and spun on his heel, heading out the door without another word. Camilla followed, hoping she wasn't making a huge mistake.

Ready or not, Texas, here I come.

CHAPTER SIX

H eath pulled the rental car alongside the large open hanger door and parked. He felt a wealth of satisfaction watching the expression of awe on Camilla's face. Throughout the drive to the small private airport where Carpenter's jet awaited them, Camilla barely spoke, though he knew her curiosity was piqued when he headed out of the city. Now she looked around the airport with wide eyes, taking in every detail. It wasn't hard to sense the excitement building in the pretty blonde. Though the flight between Charlotte and New Orleans wasn't long, maybe two hours, he planned to spoil her the entire way. A little champagne, some chocolates, and soft music might make up for the bum's rush she'd endured to get her out of town and away from whoever hunted her.

"Somehow I assumed we were flying out of Charlotte Douglas International. You plan on renting a crop duster to haul me to Texas, Goober?"

"Why didn't I think of that? If I'd known you wouldn't mind picking bugs out of your teeth, that might have been the way to go. Silly me, I thought you'd prefer a little more comfort."

Climbing from the car, he came around and opened her door, taking her hand and helping her out. Hey, he could be gallant if he wanted. Popping open the trunk, he nodded to the man standing outside the hanger doorway, who jogged over and grabbed their luggage. Heath handed him the keys and was assured the rental car would be turned in that day.

"I know I've pushed you out of your comfort zone, Cam, so let me try to make it up to you. At least a little." Heath ushered her around the corner of the hanger and heard her gasp of surprise on seeing Carpenter's fancy Gulfstream private jet. The dude was a billionaire and could afford the best, and he'd spared no expense when fitting out this beauty.

"We're flying on *that* plane?"

"Yes. My uncle pulled a few strings with a friend."

"Wow, he must be some friend."

Heath smiled at the awe in her voice and felt a surge of satisfaction he could do this for her. Give her a respite, even though it might be a brief one, away from the chaos and trauma she'd experienced over the past couple days.

A man dressed in a pilot's uniform strode forward and held out his hand. "Mr. Boudreau? I'm Arthur. Mr. Carpenter wants me to assure you the jet is at your disposal for as long as you need it. The flight plan has been filed and we are ready to leave whenever you wish." Arthur nodded to Camilla and flashed a smile. "Ms. Stewart, it's a pleasure to have you onboard. If you have any questions, or need anything, please let Chelle know. She'll being taking care of your comforts this evening. Enjoy your flight."

"Thank you, Arthur."

Heath gently took Camilla's arm and guided her to the steps leading into the plane, and watched her climb them, following closely behind. He almost echoed her gasp on entering, because there was only one word to describe the interior of the Gulfstream—decadent. Not in an overtly sexual way, though you couldn't miss the not quite subtle sensuality of the décor, but an abundance of luxury was everywhere.

"Wow. I can't seem to stop saying that, but this…" Camilla waved her hand around at the beautifully appointed interior. Thick luxurious carpet covered the entire floor, and extra-large chairs and loveseats upholstered in sinfully soft-looking leather lined both sides of the plane. Soft jazz wafted from hidden speakers, setting the exact mood Heath envisioned earlier.

"Remind me to send your friend a thank you note. This is definitely the way to travel." Camilla ran her hand over the arm of one of the chairs, stroking it, and Heath swallowed, wishing her hand was touching him instead.

"Good evening, Mr. Boudreau. Ms. Stewart. I'm Chelle. Mr. Carpenter extends his greetings, and hopes you have a pleasant flight. If you'd please take your seats and buckle in, we'll be taking off in a few moments."

"Thanks, Chelle." Camilla slid onto the seat she'd been practically fondling, instantly swallowed within its depths, and Heath took the one beside it. Reaching for her seatbelt, she swatted at his hands, and he chuckled, holding them up in mock surrender.

"Just trying to help."

"I think you've done more than enough already. Besides, I know how to buckle a seatbelt. I'm not two."

"It would have been a lot more fun if I'd done it."

"Oh, no, Bub, there's not going to be any fun on this trip. Get that thought right out of your head. I hate to burst your bubble, but I told you I have a deadline to meet, so I'm going to be at the computer pretty much all the time until this book is finished."

Heath felt the gentle rumbling vibrations of the engines and buckled his own seatbelt.

"All work and no play makes Cam—"

"Makes Cam a happy camper, because she's going to be able to retire long before she hits sixty-five. I'll have a big enough backlist I'll be able to slow down my writing schedule, and make a lovely living from it." Her grin was infectious. "Maybe I'll move to Hawaii. Buy a little place on the beach."

"Hawaii is overrated," he groused.

"Nonsense. I'm thinking warm tropical breezes as the sun sets. Sitting on the lanai with a cold drink in my hand, watching the waves roll onto the white sandy beach. No worries. No expectations. Just me and the clear blue sea. Sounds like paradise."

"In the short term, maybe. But I noticed you didn't have anybody there with you in your Hawaiian hideaway. Don't you think you'll get lonely without somebody by your side? Having the perfect getaway is nice, but without someone you love there to share it, can you really call it paradise?"

Heath watched her closely, leaning a little in her direction. He could feel the plane taxiing onto the tarmac and knew they'd be airborne within moments. Yet he waited for her answer, wondering why her idea of a tropical haven bothered him more than it should.

"I guess I never really thought about sharing my dream escape with somebody else. Probably because I never expected to find anybody I like enough to want to spend any length of time with. I haven't exactly been lucky in the love department."

"I thought you wrote romances. Doesn't that imply believing in a happily ever after?"

Camilla sighed and shifted in her seat, turning to face him. "I do believe in love. I think finding love, meeting that special someone, is one of the most amazing things in the world. I look at Tessa and your brother. Beth and your other brother. Wait, I'm sensing a pattern here." She chuckled and he joined in. "I've seen more than a few people find their special someone, and their lives turn out to be amazing. But on the flip side, I've never met anybody I clicked with, not for any length of time."

"Me either," he replied softly. "But I still believe in love. All I need is to look at Douglas and Ms. Patti. They've had more than their fair share of turmoil, raising all of us hellions. Thinking they couldn't have biological children of their own, they opened their doors and their hearts to a passel of young'uns who'd been through their own nightmares. They brought me and my brothers through things that would have most people running in the other direction, and they did it with love in their hearts for us, and a love for each other than has never dimmed. It's grown bigger and stronger through the years. That's what I want. I want what they have, a love that lasts. I won't settle for anything less."

"Wait, I thought Nica was their biological child?"

Heath grinned. "Little Miss Pampered Princess? She is. That's a long story, best told by Momma."

Before he could continue, Chelle wheeled a tray from the back of the plane. He spotted an ice bucket with a bottle of champagne and two flutes, along with a plate of fruits and cheeses, and a gold box with a big ribbon, containing what he was sure were the finest European chocolates.

"One of these days, I'm going to sit down with your mother and coerce her into telling me how she met your father. I imagine that's quite a tall tale."

"Definitely ask her. I bet she'll tell you the real story."

Heath watched her closely, wondering if she'd catch his subtle hint there was more than one story about his parents' courtship. Watched her lips quirk up in a conspiratorial grin.

"The *real* story? Oh, I love a challenge."

Heath popped the cork on the bottle of champagne and poured two glasses, handing one to Camilla. Taking a sip, she sighed and reached for the seatbelt, unclicking it and pulling her legs beneath her and reaching for one of the chocolate-covered strawberries. When her lips wrapped around the decadent treat, he swallowed the lump that had suddenly grown in his throat. The move sent a wave of need coursing through him, and he shifted, uncomfortable with the sexy thoughts racing through him.

"Is there anything you want, sweetheart?"

When her tongue peeked out and slid along her lower lip, he almost swallowed his own tongue, biting back the groan. He wanted nothing more than to haul her into his arms and kiss her, sate himself in her taste. Instead, he gulped the rest of the champagne in his glass. It was a poor substitute, but probably safer in the long run, because he had the feeling if he kissed her, he'd never stop.

"No, this is lovely. I feel like I'm being spoiled."

"You deserve a bit of pampering, especially after the last couple of days. Want some more champagne?"

She held out her glass, a mischievous glint in her eyes. "I'd love another glass, but two is my limit. Bubbly tends to go straight to my head."

"Darlin', don't you know you should never tell a man your weakness? We tend to take advantage of a confession like yours."

Camilla leaned toward him and took the glass from his hand, her fingers brushing against his, a little shock rocking him when their hands touched. This attraction to her wasn't surprising; he'd been unable to forget her since their meeting in Shiloh Springs. She'd occupied his thoughts each day and filled his erotic dream every night.

"I trust you. You'd never take advantage. Not of me."

Her words sank in, affecting him more than he cared to admit, and he suddenly felt ten feet tall. What man wouldn't when the woman he cared about said she trusted him? It felt like he'd been handed the keys to the kingdom.

"Thank you. I'll do my best to never betray that trust."

A vow he meant to keep.

Camilla raised the champagne flute to her lips, wondering why she'd blurted out those words, even though they were true. Everything she'd learned about Heath Boudreau, from when she was visiting in Texas, to talking endlessly with Beth on video chats, was positive. He was a man of honor, and though they butted heads most of the time, she had no reason not to trust him.

"I feel spoiled. This," she waved a hand toward the cart filled with treats, "it's all too much."

"You deserve a bit of pampering. Samuel Carpenter gave us free run of his jet and everything on board. It tends to be a little over-the-top, but he can afford it. The guy's got more money than he'll ever spend, and he's tricked out this baby with all the bells and whistles. His fiancée often travels with him, since she works with him at Carpenter Security. And he likes to spoil her."

She leaned her head back against the pillowy softness of the chair, indulging in the decadence. Guess the lifestyles of the rich and famous really were different than the way she lived. Of course, she could get used to this kind of luxury.

Heath reached and took the glass from her hand, setting it on the tray, and stood. "Dance with me?"

She blinked several times, not sure she'd heard him right. "But we're on a plane."

"So? There's music and plenty of room. Come on, sweetheart, dance with me. I want to hold you in my arms and forget about everything. Don't you?"

Taking a deep breath, she stood, and allowed Heath to pull her into his arms. Leaning her head against his shoulder, she relaxed and let the music fill her, swaying gently to the soft jazz pouring from the speakers.

It felt like she'd fallen into the scene from an old holiday romance movie, the kind she watched late at night, where the star would sweep the heroine off her feet in a romantic gesture, whisking her away from all her problems, to live happily ever after.

A whisper of breath against the top of her head, the warmth of his breath, had her sighing. It had been so long since she'd allowed herself to be vulnerable, to surrender herself to the moment. To simply let the world slide away and feel.

"This is nice."

"I love the way you feel in my arms, Cam."

"I don't know why, but I feel safe with you, Heath. No worries, no doubts, no fears. Safe." She slammed her lips closed. How could she have let that slip? Even if it was true.

The song continued playing, and she allowed herself to relax. This didn't need to mean anything; it could simply be a special moment out of time. She needed to remember this was temporary, and Heath would be going back to his own life once she was safe again. She needed to remember to guard her heart, keep it from breaking, because this wasn't real. Nobody would believe it if she wrote this in one of her books, because life was never soft and easy. Life wasn't a fairytale. It was cruel and ugly, difficult and rarely turned out the way you hoped and wished.

Yet for now, for this singular moment, she could pretend.

Pretend she believed in happy endings, with the heroine riding off into the sunset with the hero, deeply in love and looking forward to the future.

"Thank you," she whispered. "Thank you for caring what happens to me. For making me listen to reason, even when I don't want to."

"You never have to thank you for caring, sweetheart. I'll never let anything happen to you."

Camilla let his words wash over her, as they danced until Chelle came and told them to buckle in. They were arriving in New Orleans.

Back to reality.

CHAPTER SEVEN

Camilla smoothed a hand down her dress, surprised Heath had packed one of her favorites in his haste to get out of Charlotte. The wispy fabric fit snugly across the bosom and through the waist, and then flared over the hips to swirl around her legs. A gauzy material with flourishes of blues and greens in wavy and spiraling patterns, it made her feel utterly feminine. The only flaw in the ensemble was the lack of heels. Instead, she wore the pair of ballet flats she'd tossed in at the last second. With her hair in a messy up-do, applying mascara and a bit of lip gloss, she was ready for wherever Heath planned on taking her for dinner.

They'd arrived in New Orleans a couple of hours after leaving North Carolina. Flying on the luxurious private jet with Heath had been...wow. During the flight, they'd shared champagne and chocolates. He'd made sure she relaxed, so much so she'd actually missed their takeoff. Their subtle flirting made her feel special, even though she knew from Beth and Tessa that Heath was a notorious flirt, and she shouldn't take his sweetness and attention seriously. But it felt nice having somebody pay attention to her, catering to her needs and wants, even if his attentiveness might disappear like a puff of smoke come morning.

"Whoa."

She smiled at Heath, doing a quick spin and felt the fabric swirl around her legs. "You like?"

"You look gorgeous." He took a step forward and lifted her hand to his lips, pressing a light kiss against it. A tingle raced through her at his gesture. She had to remind herself again not to take his actions for anything more than casual flirtation. It didn't mean anything, and she'd best not read anything more into it. As attracted as she was to the big lug, she couldn't afford to risk her heart.

"Thank you." She reached onto the bed and picked up her purse, slinging the strap over her uninjured shoulder. "Were you able to get hold of your cousin?"

Heath nodded. "Ranger doesn't have a problem with us using the apartment. I figured he wouldn't, especially since Uncle Gator gave the okay. Sarah said to feel free to use any toiletries you need, since apparently I'm—and I'm quoting here—, 'a Neanderthal who probably swept you up like a Texas tornado to keep you safe' unquote."

Camilla laughed at his peeved expression, his lips pursed like he'd been sucking on a lemon. He was such a big goof, rarely taking himself seriously. Why did that appeal to her so much? "Guess she knows you pretty well."

Heath chuckled. "Not really. She's been around all the Boudreau testosterone for years. Dealing with Ranger and his brothers, not to mention the men working for Carpenter Security Services, all alpha and overprotective types, she's used to riding rein over men. Guess it runs in the Boudreau genes or something."

"Maybe it's the Boudreau name and reputation. I noticed all the Texas Boudreau men have the same traits, present company included. Though you're not blood Boudreaus, it doesn't seem to matter one wit."

"True. Guess we could debate the whole nature versus nurture argument."

"Not tonight. Much too heavy a topic for a quiet dinner. Besides, I've never been to New Orleans. I plan to absorb all the ambience and atmosphere, people and places. It'll provide good research for future books."

Heath leaned toward her and brought her hand up, placing it lightly on his crooked elbow. "My lady, your carriage awaits. There's a lovely restaurant in the French Quarter I've visited several times. Best seafood you've ever tasted."

"Can't wait. After all the goodies on the plane I shouldn't be hungry, but I'm starving. Let's go."

They took the elevator down to the ground level, and once again Camilla couldn't help being impressed by the sharp, modern décor of Carpenter Security Services office space. It took up the entire first floor of the building, and she'd noticed a couple of people earlier, including a pretty brunette manning the reception desk. She hoped there'd be time for her to do a little judicious snooping around, strictly for research. There was this series she'd been making notes for and fleshing out, and this setup would be perfect. Getting firsthand intel on the ins and outs of security work would help lend an air of authenticity. She loved it when she got her facts right for her books. Readers didn't hesitate to let her know if she got something wrong despite extensive research. No matter what anybody said, romance readers were some of the most well-educated, intelligent people she'd ever met, and she loved it.

"You might hear some noises down here, even with the apartment being soundproofed. These guys can get loud, believe me."

"I love Ranger's place. He's lucky to have an apartment so close to everything in New Orleans. I know this area is prime real estate, especially being so close to the French Quarter."

"Yeah, he can thank Samuel Carpenter for that. When Carpenter moved his headquarters from Dallas back to New Orleans, he renovated an old building his grandfather left him. It had been in the family for generations. He had the place completely redone from top to bottom, outfitting the lower level to contain his security company, and the upper floors were converted into apartments. If he's around while we are here, I'll show up the rooftop deck. The view is spectacular. You can see the city, and the bridge over the Mississippi lit up at night is stunning."

"I'd love that."

Heath opened the front door, leading Camilla out to the street, where a large town car with a driver waited at the curb.

"Carpenter didn't stop there," he added, helping her into the car before sliding onto the seat beside her. "He's a good friend of the family, has been since he was a kid. He had an apartment set aside for all four of my cousins, all of whom work for the company. Each one got their own place, totally paid for, lock, stock, and barrel. All they had to do was move in. He made the same arrangement for my cousin, Gabi, though she didn't want to be in the same building with her brothers. After she graduated from college and spread her wings figuring out what she wanted to do, Carpenter got her and her fiancé a place close to the French Quarter."

"Talk about generous. I could use a benefactor like that. The mortgage payments on my townhouse eat up a large chunk of my royalties every month. Hmm, maybe I should look for a sugar daddy, to keep me in the style I'd like to become accustomed to." She grinned, letting him know she was joking.

"I wouldn't plan on using your feminine wiles on Carpenter. No offense, but his fiancée would wipe the floor with you, sugar, and you'd never see it coming. She's former CIA, a fully trained operative. They're getting married soon."

Camilla chuckled softly, letting him know in a roundabout way she got the message. Not that she had any intention of making advances on anybody—except maybe him. The more time she spent around him, the more she liked what she saw. For such a large man, he was surprisingly tender. During the flight, she'd learned they shared quite a few of the same interests, had a similar sense of humor, and he never tried to intimidate or overwhelm her. Oh, she knew he was strong, physically and emotionally, but he seemed to know exactly how far he could push her without stepping over the line, a fact she credited to his mother. Having met Ms. Patti, she knew exactly who ruled the Boudreau men with an iron fist.

"So, you mentioned the restaurant you're taking me to is in the French Quarter?"

He leaned back against the plush leather seat and picked up her hand, tracing his thumb across the back in a soft gesture. "I thought we might walk through the Quarter a bit before we eat. Or we can eat first, if you'd like."

"I don't mind looking around first. Maybe you can point out the interesting landmarks, or the quirky stuff only a local would know. This city has always fascinated me, and I'm looking forward to learning more about it."

The car pulled to a stop close to Jackson Brewery on Decatur Street, and Heath helped her from the car. Camilla knew she looked like a gawky tourist, but everything was so different from Charlotte. Not that North Carolina didn't have its unique charms, but she'd always loved seeing pictures and reading about New Orleans. Everything about the city fascinated her. If she'd known she was coming, she'd have made a list of all the things she wanted to see and do. A carriage ride in the French Quarter. Going on a ghost tour through the cemetery. Seeing all the artists around Jackson Square painting and selling their works. At least tonight, she'd get to fulfill one of the things on her impromptu bucket list: eating in a New Orleans restaurant.

"Jackson's Brewery has been a landmark in New Orleans for decades." Heath leaned closer and whispered in her ear. "It's evolved into everything from a restaurant to a wedding and special events venue now. Plus, there are condos, you name it. But the building itself is impressive."

Heath grasped her hand again, threading his fingers through hers, and she felt a tingle race through her. He seemed to like holding her hand. In the car on the trip over, he'd played with her fingers almost absently. While she hadn't pictured him as one who'd necessarily be comfortable with public displays of affection, he ignored everyone around them, focusing his attention solely on her as they walked down the street and headed into the more formal French Quarter.

"It can get a little loud the farther in you get," he leaned closer as he spoke, and she caught the slightest hint of his aftershave. "If you look right there," he gestured with his right hand, "you can see the Mississippi River."

She stopped and spun in the direction he'd pointed, and her mouth dropped open. There it was in all its glory, the most famous river in the United States. There was a huge bridge spanning the majestic sight, and now that she was listening closely, she heard the sounds of boats. Taking a deep breath, the tang of briny air filled her senses, and she turned toward Heath.

"I can't believe I'm in New Orleans, standing this close to the Mississippi." She practically vibrated with excitement, her mind racing with story possibilities. It was an occupational hazard: being a writer, she was also cataloging sights and sounds and places for use later.

"She's a beautiful old city. Once everything has been resolved, and you're safe, you'll have to come back and explore at your leisure. There's far too much to see, and we're only going to be here for a little while."

Heath's words brought reality crashing back, dimming her excitement for a second or two, before she decided she wasn't about to allow some nameless, faceless enemy to destroy this moment. She was in one place she'd fantasized about visiting, and she was seeing it with a man she'd had more than her fair share of sexy dreams about. Nobody was going to rain on her parade.

"Let's go. I want to see everything."

Heath laughed, his joy rippling across her skin like a physical caress. She needed to put the brakes on her feelings before things progressed past the point of no return. Falling for the big, brawny cowboy would be the biggest mistake she could make, because there wasn't a chance in creation he wouldn't end up breaking her heart.

As they walked, he started pointing out little hidden gems along their route. Little mom and pop shops, the voodoo priestess store tucked away around a darkened corner. They walked in amiable silence, her hand still tucked in his. Music painted the air with jazz played by street corner musicians, and people danced in the streets with utter abandon, wrapped up in the magic the city imbued. The vibe of freedom and *joie de vivre* was alive and well in the Big Easy.

When his phone trilled, Heath pulled it from his pocket and looked at the screen, a frown forming little lines across his forehead. Without missing a beat, he shoved it back into his pocket and kept walking, gently tugging her along with him.

"Who was that?"

"It wasn't anything important."

She stopped, digging in her heels when he tried to keep going. "Don't lie to me. From your frown, it wasn't news you wanted to hear. If you need to call them back, let's find a place that's a little quieter, and you can make the call."

"We're almost at the restaurant. Let's get a table, and I'll call them back then."

Walking another block, Heath pointed to a restaurant set back off of Bourbon Street, hidden down an alley, away from the boisterous crowd. With a hand on her back, he guided her through the front door. Within mere seconds, they were led to a table on the patio. The courtyard was enclosed with wrought iron fencing, decorative and intricate, giving the illusion of privacy. The sounds coming off Bourbon Street were muted this far back, and Camilla felt like she'd stepped into her own little corner of paradise.

"This place is beautiful. Exactly what I picture when I think about a New Orleans restaurant."

"My Uncle Gator recommended this place to me years ago, when I spent a few months on a job for the ATF. He knows the owners. Of course, he knows just about everybody in the city. He's a bit of a local legend."

"I guess you've been here a lot."

"Not as much as I'd like. When I'm working, I tend to be more of a grab some fast food on the way to my hotel room type. The food here is excellent, though."

A white-shirted waiter appeared at their table, holding a bottle of wine, and Heath nodded. The bottle was quickly uncorked and poured, and the waiter disappeared. The deep redness of the wine under the sparkling lights overhead tempted Camilla, and she picked up her glass.

"I know I haven't said it, but thank you. I'm still having a hard time believing somebody is after me. I wish I could wrap my head around what I did or said, or what they think I know to make them want to hurt me." She took a sip of the wine, feeling its warmth spread through her.

"We'll figure it out. I've got people working on it."

"I appreciate it. You didn't have to do any of this. I'm not your responsibility. I mean, we hardly know each other."

Camilla lowered her gaze, not wanting to see pity in Heath's eyes.

"Cam, it wasn't that I didn't want to get to know you better. Meeting you in Shiloh Springs...let's simply say you got under my skin. But long-distance relationships rarely work out, and I didn't want to drag you into my life."

"I know. When we met, I wasn't in a great place mentally. Evan had been giving me fits about signing some papers my parents needed. He's my brother, but I'm not oblivious to his faults. I hate what he did to Beth and Jamie, the agony he's put them both through. I feel kind of responsible, because I grew up with him. I should have known what he was capable of, but he fooled everybody. Even me."

"Your brother's actions are his alone. There's nothing for you to be sorry for; you didn't know what he planned, or you'd have stopped him. You aren't the kind of person who'd stand idly by while people you cared about were in danger."

She took another sip of wine and studied Heath closely. Maybe he understood her better than she thought. Opening her mouth, she started to ask him a question, but the ringing of his phone interrupted. Shoot, she'd forgotten about his call a few minutes earlier, the one she'd urged him to return.

"I'm sorry, I really need to handle this. Be right back."

He walked several feet away, to stand beside the decorative fencing enclosing the patio, and she wanted for several moments while he spoke quietly to whoever was on the other end, then listened intently. Everything about him screamed alpha male, from his size to his obvious affection for those he cared about. She got the feeling maybe she was being added into that select few, too.

Wanting to capture the moment, because she might never get the chance to come back to New Orleans, she pulled her cell phone from her bag and turned it on. She'd powered if off earlier for the flight. Turning on the camera app, she snapped several pictures of the patio, trying to capture its beauty and the unique blend of French and Creole culture in the ambience. She snapped the metalwork fence, the white bulbs illuminating the courtyard, the flameless candles burning in holders on the individual tables. The patio wasn't crowded, with a smattering of people spread out, enjoying the evening air.

She heard Heath before she saw him, and he snatched the phone from her hand, scowling at her.

"What?"

"Are you insane?" He shook his head before shutting off her phone. "My fault. I meant to give you a burner phone on the plane, but forgot." With deft movements, he popped open the back of her phone and slid the battery free, then put the back on.

"What are you doing?"

"You can't use your phone. Anybody with half a brain can trace your location via your GPS. We're going to have to move again faster than I'd hoped."

"Darn it, I never even considered that. I should have. Such a stupid move."

"Not your fault. I keep forgetting you're not used to having your life turned upside down. Remind me when we get back to the apartment to give you a burner phone to use until things get back to normal." He handed her the phone and the battery he'd removed."

She stared at her phone for several seconds before tossing it and the battery into her purse. "My whole life is on that phone. Names and phone numbers, contact information. Book ideas. Photos I take for reference and research. I can't afford to lose any of it."

"You won't. My brother, Ridge, has a computer genius who works for him. She'll be able to backup all your data onto the burner phone and give you a copy you can upload to your computer."

"Cool. Can I ask, and don't get all testy at the question, is this computer genius a hacker? Because I'd really like to interview a hacker—for research."

Heath burst out laughing, his shoulders shaking. "I'll have Ridge ask Destiny if she'll talk with you while you're in Shiloh Springs."

"Excellent."

Reaching across the table, she took his hand and squeezed it. "I'm sorry for making such a bonehead move. Do you want to leave now and head for your ranch?"

He shook his head, though he reversed their hold, her

hand now secured in his. "No, let's go ahead and have dinner. We don't know for sure anybody's tracking your phone, and it wasn't on that long. We'll head for Texas in the morning."

"Thanks." She gave him a cheeky grin. "Besides, I'm starving. Any recommendations?"

"You can't go wrong with anything here, it's all delicious."

"Mr. Heath?" A feminine voice came from over Camilla's left shoulder, and she saw Heath grin.

"Adele, my love, how are you?" Heath stood and embraced a tiny gray-haired woman whose head barely reached the slope of his shoulders. Bending forward, he placed a kiss against her weathered skin, and she stood on her tiptoes and patted his cheek.

"Can't complain. Business is good, though you haven't stopped by in forever. How are Gator and Ms. Willie?"

"They're doing well. Gator's complaining because Ms. Willie's baking is making him fat and sassy."

"Jacques and I are pleased he found somebody who loves him. Tell them to come by soon."

"I will, Adele." Heath gestured toward Camilla. "May I introduce my good friend, Camilla Stewart. Camilla, this gorgeous woman is Adele Benoit, one of the owners. I keep trying to get her to run away with me, but she refuses to leave her husband."

Camilla smiled at his gentle flirting with the older woman, whose cheeks had turned a lovely pink. "It's a pleasure to meet you, Mrs. Benoit."

"Please, you must call me Adele. Any friend of my Heath's is welcome here. Have you decided on what you'd like, or shall I have Jacques send you out something special?"

Camilla raised a brow at Heath, and he shrugged. "Everything Jacques cooks is superb. Tell him Camilla has never been to New Orleans before, and we need to make a good impression, so she'll want to come back."

"*Mais oui.* We have a lovely crawfish etouffee tonight with fresh crispy bread. Jacques also made sausage Boudin earlier as a starter. Maybe a lovely white chocolate bread pudding with a bourbon and pecan sauce to finish?"

"That sounds amazing." Camilla could almost feel her stomach rumbling as the food was described. Knowing she'd be eating authentic New Orleans cooking made it even better. Though she wished she had her cell, so she could take photos to remember sharing this special meal with Heath.

"Sounds perfect, Adele. Thank you."

"I'll check back with you later. Anything you need, you tell Benny, your server. I'll make sure he knows to take good care of you and your lady."

As Adele walked away, Heath returned to his seat, grinning. "You've just seen Cajun hospitality at work. Adele and her husband have been running this place for decades. It's a local institution, though it's getting more and more popular with the tourist set."

"She's a wonderful hostess. I definitely feel welcome." She lifted her glass higher. "Thank you for bringing me here. By the way, did you get to finish your call before I had the whole screw up with the phone?"

He gave an abrupt nod. "It was my office in DC. We needed to clear up my taking a few days off."

Camilla felt her heart drop into her stomach. "I knew it. Your helping me is causing you problems. Listen, I can get to Shiloh Springs alone. I'll rent a car and drive—"

"Stop. Everything is fine. As a matter of fact, my boss asked me to look into something for him while I'm in Texas. So, in reality, I'm actually on the job."

"Are you sure? I'd hate to be the cause of you losing your job."

His burst of laughter surprised her. "Sweetheart, that's one thing you don't need to worry about, I'm in no danger of being fired. Trust me, the ATF is pleased with my job performance. This is simply a small hiccup; they know I'll be back to work soon enough."

Their waiter approached with a platter of something that smelled divine, and placed it in the center of the table. Remoulade and a Cajun mustard dipping sauce accompanied the Boudin.

"Dig in," Heath said, motioning toward the plate. "I promise you won't be disappointed."

Camilla broke one of the balls apart and dipped it into the remoulade and popped it into her mouth. She closed her eyes as the flavors burst upon her tongue, and she heard a soft moan escape. Swallowing the first bite, she opened her eyes and caught the look of hunger on Heath's face, one which had nothing to do with food. Heat flooded into her cheeks.

"It's amazing. I could eat this every day and never get tired of it."

"The variety of food in The Big Easy is known world-wide, for good reason. It would take a lifetime to sample everything this city has to offer." He popped a piece into his mouth and chewed.

Now she'd had her first taste, she tried the other dipping sauce, and decided she couldn't pick a favorite because they were both different and delicious, Camilla could hardly wait for the next course. When the etouffee came, she dug in, relishing every bite. She was stuffed by the time she'd finished her last bite.

"You're going to have to roll me back to the apartment, because I don't think I'm going to be able to walk on my own."

"You'll make it, I promise. Tell me you don't have a little bit of room for dessert."

No sooner had he spoke the words, than the bread pudding slid into place before her. She wasn't sure where she was going to put it, but there was no way she wasn't taking at least a bite or two of the decadent dessert.

Heath dug his spoon into the one in front of him, making sure to get some of the whiskey pecan sauce along with the white chocolate, and held the temptation in front of her lips.

"Come on, sweetheart, one bite. You won't regret it, I promise."

The sultry tone underlying his words made her think he was talking about more than dessert, but she couldn't resist. She didn't want to. Opening her mouth, she let him slide the spoonful of sinful goodness inside, and she licked it clean.

"Was I right?"

She nodded instead of answering, staring into his brilliant blue eyes. If she let him, he'd seduce her into more than indulging in a whiskey-soaked temptation. Was she ready for that?

Steeling herself, she broke eye contact, concentrating instead on her own bowl. She managed to eat almost half before pushing it away. "I can't eat another bite."

"Did you enjoy your first meal in New Orleans?"

"I can't imagine anything better. This meal, letting me wander around and do the tourist thing, it's been amazing. I'm sorry we have to leave in the morning. I'm sorry I screwed up, and ruined everything."

Heath waved for the check, and the waiter rushed forward and whispered something, low enough she couldn't hear. Standing, he walked around the table, and helped her to her feet.

"It's probably for the best. It would be too easy to give in to the chemistry between us, and it's too soon. But mark my works, Ms. Camilla, once we've made sure you are safe, we're going to explore this thing between us. Don't try and deny it. You felt the same pull as I did when we were in Shiloh Springs a few months ago. Now I've seen you again, gotten to know you a little more, I'm not going to fight this pull, this attraction, any longer. I want to see where it leads, don't you?"

Camilla rolled his words around, feeling them, tasting them, hearing the sincerity underlying what he said. Did she really want to fight the attraction she'd felt from the moment she'd seen him? Who knows, maybe once she had her life back on track, they could see if making a long-distance relationship work.

"Yes. When everything is back to some semblance of normal, I want to see where this leads. No running, no hiding, because that's my usual reaction. I want to give *us* a shot."

Heath's heated smile sent tingles racing down her spine, and Camilla mentally crossed her fingers, because she had the feeling she was in for a bumpy ride.

CHAPTER EIGHT

The sun had barely peeked over the horizon when Heath started the coffee. He stretched, feeling the muscles pull in his lower back. Camilla had taken the main bedroom, and he'd ended up on the couch, since the second bedroom was a kid's room for Ranger and Sarah's daughter. He'd gotten spoiled having a comfy bed to come home to most nights in his apartment in Arlington, or maybe he was too old to be sleeping on a lumpy sofa.

He'd tossed and turned most of the night; his brain wouldn't shut down. The pressing thought of who was after Camilla repeated itself over and over, yet he couldn't find any rhyme or reason for someone to be after her. From everything she had told him, and from what Officer Dandridge was able to piece together, there wasn't a single reason anybody would try to hurt her, much less take her life.

Heath was good at puzzles. Enjoyed figuring out the intricacies and details of piecing clues together, determining where each piece went until he could view the entire picture with clarity. Except this particular puzzle seemed to have a whole lot of missing components, and until he figured out where the individual pieces interlocked, he couldn't determine what the whole picture was, and it drove him crazy.

He leaned his shoulder against the exposed brick by the large window, and watched the skyline as dawn painted the sky with vivid hues, and drew in a ragged breath. It wouldn't be long before he'd have to wake Camilla, and hit the road for Shiloh Springs. Besides, it was his fault. He'd been so wrapped up in Cam, he'd forgotten about confiscating her phone. It was a stupid rookie mistake; one he prayed wouldn't cost them.

"Heath?"

Turning, he spotted Camilla standing at the end of the hall, dressed in a pretty feminine sleepshirt with lace edging along her collarbones, the deep blue color highlighting her tousled blonde hair spilling over her shoulders. She looked like she'd just tumbled out of bed after a night in the arms of a lover, sleepy eyed and still gorgeous, and sweetly innocent wrapped in a decadent package. Darn, if he didn't wish he could sweep her off her feet and carry her back to bed.

"Morning, sunshine. Hope you got a good night's sleep, because we're hitting the road soon."

"Not without coffee. If you want me awake enough to function, I'm gonna need a large infusion of caffeine."

He smiled. "It should be ready any time. You want breakfast?"

"Ugh, no. I can't eat first thing when I wake up. Coffee and e-mails are my morning routine. I don't mind if you want something though."

"I only eat breakfast when I'm in Shiloh Springs, and that's only because Momma would have a conniption fit if I tried to leave the house without fueling up. I'm more of a grab a large coffee and a doughnut on the way to work kind of guy."

She sauntered past him into the kitchen, and reached up into the cupboard, exposing a long length of sexy leg, and Heath swallowed past the lump in his throat. This was why he'd avoided spending any time with her. The pull the woman had on him was inexplicable. He'd dated his fair share before and after he'd left Texas. Shoot, probably more than his share, if he was honest. He wasn't a hound dog, but he loved women. A little feminine company helped make being away from home tolerable. Yet not a single one of them made him feel the way Camilla did with a simple smile or the touch of her hand in his.

He was a goner, and there wasn't a thing he could do about it. Fighting the attraction hadn't worked. Goodness knows he'd tried. Distance only made things harder. His daddy told him long ago when he met the right woman, he'd know it immediately, like being struck by lightning, instantaneous and no denying it. Maybe he should have listened to his old man, because fighting the overwhelming need to be with Camilla hadn't worked. Every single day since he'd met her at the big house, he'd done his damnedest to keep her from getting under his skin.

Now he knew better, because she'd burrowed straight into his heart, and he wasn't fighting it anymore.

She pulled two coffee mugs out, sat them next to the coffeemaker, and began searching for the sugar bowl. Heath had noted she liked her coffee on the sweet side, and heard her sigh of relief as she found it. Picking the coffee pot up, she filled the two cups and handed him one. After adding several spoons of sweetener to hers, she leaned her hip against the counter and took a long swallow.

"We've got time for a shower if you want one before we leave. Uncle Gator dropped off a car for us last night. It'll get us to Shiloh Springs and should be untraceable. It's one of the undercover cars Carpenter Security uses for stakeouts, so it's rather unremarkable in appearance, but he assures me the engine can fly."

"Your family seems to be good at overcoming pretty insurmountable obstacles without breaking a sweat. I still have nightmares about Evan kidnapping Jamie, yet all the Boudreaus rallied around, came up with a plan to get her back, and implemented everything perfectly. Must be a family trait."

"We've had a lot of experience overcoming some insurmountable obstacles. But we've had some mighty fine living examples. Uncle Gator raised his four sons and his daughter with the same morals and integrity that Douglas and Ms.

Patti taught us. Our Uncle Hank taught his family, too. Having those things ingrained into our everyday life, seeing those living examples being true to their teachings, it changes you in fundamental ways. Maybe someday I'll tell you how much living with Dad and Momma changed me."

"I'd like that."

He couldn't help watching the way she kept glancing his way through half-lowered lids, or the sweet blush that stained her cheeks. As much as they needed to hit the road, he wished they had another day or two, maybe get to spend some quiet time simply talking and getting to know each other. Instead, it seemed every minute since she'd been shot had been packed with a frenetic mishmash of activity.

When he looked at her arm, he noted the bandage was missing. The area where the bullet had grazed her skin looked fine. A little pink along the edges, but that was to be expected with a traumatic injury. The larger bandage on her forehead had been replaced with a Band-Aid, the color blending into her skin tone and making it almost disappear from a distance.

"How's your arm feeling? The stitches giving you any problems?"

Camilla glanced over at her arm, frowning. "It's okay. A little stiff when I got up, but overall, nothing I can't handle. And before you ask, yes, I'm taking my antibiotics."

"What about the pain med? Do you need it?"

She shook her head. "It doesn't bother me enough to

need it."

Heath's phone rang, and he walked over to the coffee table in front of the sofa where he'd laid it, looking at the caller ID. "I need to take this."

"I'll go and grab a shower and get dressed." She carried her coffee cup with her down the hall and Heath watched the gentle sway of her hips as she walked away and sighed before answering the call.

"Hey, bro. What's up?"

"Me, that's what's up at this ungodly hour. Do you know what time it is in Portland?" Shiloh's aggravated tone had Heath smiling. His brother wasn't known for being Mr. Bright and Chipper first thing in the morning.

"Yes, I know what time it is in Portland. Why are you calling *me* this early?"

Shiloh's sigh was audible over the phone. "I'm frustrated and need to vent. I swear, it's like Renee's taunting me, begging me to catch her. Every time I get close, her trail vanishes like a bloody puff of smoke. It's almost like she's psychic, because I don't know how she figures out when I get close."

"Maybe she is."

"Is what?"

Heath chuckled at his brother's aggravated tone. "Maybe she is psychic. And before you start, yep, I know ninety-nine percent of those claiming some kind of ability are charlatans and frauds. But I've met one or two people who have a genuine gift. Remember the woman Uncle Gator told us about here in New Orleans? The one who's married to the private investigator? She's the real deal.

"Whoa, wait a second. Did you say *here* in New Orleans? What are you doing there, bro?"

"Have you talked to the folks recently?"

"No. I've been up here running around like an idiot, trying to catch up to Renee or Elizabeth. It's hard to keep the name straight. I've got the feeling she's going to be bolting soon, leaving the city. Probably changing her name again. Why?"

Heath breathed in a deep breath before answering. "Camilla's gotten herself in a bit of a bind, and I'm playing bodyguard. And before you ask, no, I don't need you to come and help. I've got things covered. We're on our way to Shiloh Springs, just taking a bit of a circuitous route."

There was a long moment of silence before Shiloh asked, "What kind of trouble are we talking about? I can do some digging from this end. I've got my computer and my contacts, all at your disposal, if you need me."

The corners of Heath's lips tilted upward. He wasn't surprised by his brother's offer of help. Pretty much every single one of his brothers offered their assistance before he'd caught the plane to North Carolina. Even Nica had offered to drop everything and go with him, assuring him she wouldn't have any problem missing a few classes.

I really love my family.

"Thanks, but you concentrate on finding Renee. We've looked for her for so long, and this is the first time anybody's gotten this close. Focus on bringing her home. I can handle Camilla."

He heard an outraged harrumph behind him and glanced over his shoulder to see Camilla standing with her hands on her hips, glaring at him. Great, now he'd have to explain his comment. Though at the twinkle in her eyes, maybe he wouldn't.

"You sure?"

"We're heading for the Big House in a few minutes. Uncle Gator loaned us one of Carpenter's undercover cars, so we shouldn't catch a tail. Once we hit Shiloh Springs, I'm betting the family circles the wagons and nobody's getting past them to take another shot at her."

"Wait, somebody shot at Camilla? I thought when you said you were playing bodyguard, you meant simply doing babysitting duty, chauffeuring her around, trying to gain a few brownie points with your gal. Truthfully, bro, how serious is this?"

Heath scratched his chin, felt the raspy growth, and wondered if he had time for a shave before they headed out. "Don't know yet. Somebody took a shot at her outside her townhouse. Bullet scraped her arm, and a possible second one tore a groove in her forehead. Brought her home from the hospital and found a rattler in her bed."

Out of the corner of his eye, Heath watched Camilla

pour another cup of coffee and add a ton of sugar, turn and give him a wink, before sitting on one of the dining chairs. She seemed to be handling everything pretty well this morning, all things considered, he mused.

"Are you even listening to me?" Shiloh's voice was filled with amusement. "Or did Camilla walk into the room and your tongue's hanging on the floor?"

"Yes, yes, and yes. Call me if you find anything about Renee or if you need me."

"I will. I'm only a call away if things get hairy."

Heath chuckled at Shiloh's lack of a goodbye. He'd bet his mind was already on his hunt for their brother's sister, though he'd always thought of Renee as his sister too, even though they'd never met.

"Who's Renee?" Camilla's sweet smile didn't quite reach her eyes, and Heath had the fleeting impression she was jealous. Yeah, right.

"Renee is Lucas' younger sister. They were separated when they were kids and put into the foster care system. We've been looking for her for a long time. Finally got a promising lead. Shiloh's on the west coast, in Portland, following up to see if we might be able to reunite them."

Her eyes widened. "That's a long time to be looking for one person."

He nodded and stood, walking into the kitchen and refilling his cup. "She's family."

"Wouldn't the state have records? Once children go into

the foster system, they are required to keep meticulous records on every move that child makes, until they're eighteen. I did a lot of research on this for a book. Unfortunately, there are kids that fall through the cracks, some are runaways, others end up in the grasp of human traffickers or drugs. But she couldn't just fall off the face of the earth."

"All the records are gone. Nothing in the state's database. Zilch. Ditto on any paper records. The office where her case was handled for the first couple of years burned to the ground in the midst of their files being transferred into the computer system. Lucas was told there was a backlog of paperwork, but I think that's a crock. I think it's a little too coincidental. Sometimes a coincidence is a coincidence, and sometimes it's somebody having something to hide."

Camilla took a sip of her coffee, staring into space, and he wondered what she was thinking. She had a sharp brain and intelligence to spare. He loved her mind and her creativity. During the night, he'd downloaded one of her books and read it, unable to put it down once he started. That was the other reason, besides the cramped sofa, he hadn't slept. The way she made every scene come alive intrigued him, and the emotion shared between the hero and heroine was hot and steamy.

"Any idea if she got adopted? Or did she remain in foster care?"

Heath shook his head. "We haven't found any adoption records filed in Texas or anywhere else. Lucas has been searching for years. Ever clue he gets, it's like one step forward and two steps back. With some help from Dad's army buddies, there was a lead in Cincinnati. By the time he got there, she'd ghosted."

"That's awful. My heart's breaking for him. I can't imagine knowing you have a sibling out in the world somewhere, somebody you love, and having no way to contact them."

"It's the reason Lucas never changed his last name, on the off chance Renee might be looking for him. He's a Boudreau in every way that matters, and Momma and Dad fully agreed with his decision." Heath took a drink of his coffee before continuing. "It was a fluke how we got the lead on Renee, or Elizabeth. That was the name she used in Cincinnati. Personally, I think she had to get out of town so fast she never had the chance to change her ID, so she's using the same name in Portland."

"What happened?"

"I got assigned a newbie with the agency. Young buck who'd transferred in from Portland, Oregon. Working a stakeout and shooting the bull when he mentioned this girl he'd been seeing before he got transferred to Virginia. She'd moved into the apartment building where he lived, and they'd talked a bit. I felt like I'd been hit by an eighteen-wheeler when he mentioned the girl's name."

Camilla's eyes lit up at this attempt at humor. "Lemme guess, Elizabeth."

"Ding, ding, ding. Give the girl a prize. Same first and

last name. Description matched. Chuck even had a picture, one of her working out in the building's gym. She looks like Lucas. It can't be a coincidence. Same auburn hair, same features. Unless Renee has a doppelgänger, it's her."

Camilla's eyes widened. "Shoot. If you didn't have to babysit me, you'd be in Portland right now, wouldn't you?"

"Stop. I'm exactly where I want to be. Lucas couldn't leave. Shiloh volunteered to check into the tip, see if it's really her." Heath chuckled and leaned back in the chair, linking his hands on his stomach. "She's giving him fits, running him ragged. He plans on questioning her as soon as he can pin her down in one place long enough. Better happen sooner rather than later because he feels she's about to bolt."

"I hope he finds out it's really her. Beth told me Lucas and Jill are finally together. It would be awesome if he reunited with his long-lost sister, too."

Heath smiled at the wistful tone in her voice. "I love seeing my brother so happy. It's been hard, living so far away from them, but the last few times I talked to Lucas, he'd seemed—distant. I think his heart wasn't in the big city anymore. Plus, he'd been pining for Jill, though he'd never have admitted it. It took some work, true, and a bit of matchmaking on my mother's part, but he finally realized what he'd been missing all along."

Camilla stared into her coffee cup. "Want some breakfast before we leave? I can cook something."

"Might be better if we grabbed something on the road. It'll take several hours to drive to Shiloh Springs, and I want to get us there. I'll feel a lot better once we're at the ranch."

She stood and rinsed her coffee cup. "I'll go get dressed. I won't be long."

Heath watched her stride down the hall to the bedroom, and felt a tinge of regret that her life had been disrupted. Turned upside-down by some idiot with a gun. Dandridge better pray he caught whoever was after Camilla before Gator found out who was behind the attempt on her life. Gator wouldn't hesitate to contact Heath once he finished his search for the culprit. Then the real hunt would begin, and Heath wouldn't hesitate in eliminating anyone who threatened Camilla. No matter what it took.

CHAPTER NINE

Camilla woke with a start, snapping forward against her seatbelt with a gasp, the breath forced in and out of her lungs in labored breaths. Her heart raced, feeling like it wanted to leap from her chest. The remnants of the nightmare lingered, before fading into the ether, and she closed her eyes, trying to hold onto it.

"You okay?"

She stared out the windshield, watching the scenery race past, and deliberately slowed her breathing. "I had a nightmare. I dreamed about being shot again."

"Again? You mean a different shooting from the one that actually happened?"

"Huh, I guess so." She tried replaying elements of the dream. Remembered standing in front of her townhouse. Something drew her outside. What was it? Squeezing her eyes tight, she concentrated, grasping at the remnants of the dream before it faded away completely.

"Can you remember your dream? Maybe if we talk about it, you'll feel better."

"I was standing outside my townhouse. I—something

caused me to be there, but I don't remember what. I stood outside the gate, facing the parking area. I remember an SUV parked in front of my house. That's not unusual. My neighbor uses it all the time since I don't have a car. I don't remember him having an SUV, but this was a dream, so..."

"Was it daytime or nighttime?"

She scrunched her brow, before answering. "It wasn't dark, but I have the feeling it wasn't morning, either. So, maybe midafternoon?" A road sign slid into view, showing they'd already crossed the border into Texas.

How long have I been asleep?

"Keep going, sweetheart."

"The next thing I know, I'm lying on the sidewalk bleeding, with my hands over my stomach. There's blood everywhere, spilling over my hands, between my fingers. I can feel its warmth. It's sticky. I tried screaming, but nothing came out. Barely a sound, not matter how hard I tried. When I tried to sit up, hands reached for me, pulling at me. I fought, struggling against their grip, because I knew if they took me, I'd never be seen again."

"You're right, that's definitely a nightmare. Could you see anybody's face? Hear their voice?"

Camilla shook her head. "It's funny, I didn't hear anything now that you said it. No traffic. No birds chirping. Nothing."

"In your dream, did you hear the shot?"

"Now that you mention it, no, I don't remember hearing

it."

"How did you feel before you were shot? What emotions were going through you?" Heath glanced at her, then lifted one hand off the wheel and squeezed her hand lightly.

"I don't know." She scrubbed her hands across her face and fought the urge to scream. The nightmare images were fading. "I can't remember anything else." She slapped her fist against her leg. "I'm sick of not being able to remember. Somebody who I can't put a name or a face to is turning my life upside down. Why are they doing this? Who hates me enough they'd want to hurt me?"

"I don't think anybody hates you, Cam. You're sweet and kind and loving. No, this is about something else, which is what we need to figure out." He paused for several seconds before asking, "Have any of your memories come back? Maybe the nightmare triggered something?"

Closing her eyes, she concentrated, thinking back to before the actual shooting. Nothing was different. The memories of dinner with her parents, arguing with them and heading home remained the same. Then nothing but a big empty hole until she woke up in the emergency room.

"I hate this! It's like somebody stole a part of me, and I feel lesser. None of this makes sense. I keep asking myself why. Why me?"

"We'll figure it out. Dandridge is working the case on his end, and whether he likes it or not, he'll be getting a little assistance from my uncle. Uncle Gator can ferret out a clue like a bloodhound on the scent. He's on his way to North Carolina right now. Trust me, he'll dig until we get answers."

"Now I feel even worse. I'm disrupting people's lives. Tell him not to go."

"Yeah, right. Trying to tell Gator Boudreau not to do something once he's made his mind up is like trying to keep the tide from rolling in. Uncle Gator is the proverbial White Knight. Damsels in distress are his specialty." She caught the quirky grin on his face, before he added, "Kinda like me."

"Known a lot of damsels in your time, have you?"

"My fair share."

Camilla snorted. "I bet you have, Goober."

"We've got another couple of hours before we hit Shiloh Springs. Why don't you try to get some rest? You're sure to be bombarded by people as soon as we get there, especially Beth and Momma."

She took a deep cleansing breath. "Good idea." Shifting to find a comfortable spot, she closed her eyes and drifted to sleep, hoping the nightmare didn't come back.

Hours later, Heath pulled onto the drive leading to the Big House, filled with the sense of coming home. It didn't matter if he'd been gone for a day or a year, an overwhelming sensation of peace and welcome suffused him every time he turned onto the ranch. Rolling down the driver's window, he inhaled the rarefied air of a warm Texas afternoon and smiled.

Camilla stretched and shifted in the passenger seat. Luckily, she'd managed to nap most of the way after her nightmare, only waking when they'd driven through downtown Shiloh Springs.

"I swear there's something about this place. It feels like I'm being enveloped in a big warm hug. It happened the first time I came to visit Beth and Jamie. I've never felt anything like it before. Even you, with your obnoxious tormenting and laptop stealing ways, didn't alleviate the warmth and welcome I felt the first time I visited."

"Funny, I was thinking the same thing. Whenever I'm away, when I come back it feels like the ranch is welcoming me back. I hadn't thought about it feeling like a hug, but that describes it perfectly. It's coming home."

It took a couple minutes before they reached the front of the Big House. They found several cars parked like little tin soldiers standing at attention at the front of the house. Guess Momma rounded up whatever family was in town. Heath wasn't sure how he felt about it, worried it might put them in the crosshairs. Then again, the more people keeping watch over Camilla, the better. Especially since she couldn't remember who was after her.

"That's a lot of cars."

"Yeah, looks like Momma's been rallying the troops. Bet

they're all inside, stuffing their faces and waiting for us to show up." He smiled, before adding, "Brody's truck is here, so Beth and Jamie probably are, too."

"Woohoo!" Camilla flung her door open before he'd even unbuckled his seatbelt and headed for the front steps.

"Hang on, darlin'," was the most he got out before a herd of bodies swarmed onto the front porch. Beth met Camilla on the steps, wrapping her in a big hug.

"Are you okay?" Beth leaned back and looked at Camilla, studying her intently. It was impossible not to see the love between the two women. Or the worry in Beth's eyes. Even though the tie between them rested solely through Jamie, Camilla and Beth acted like sisters. Pretty amazing, he thought, seeing what Evan Stewart had put them both through.

"I'm fine. The arm doesn't hurt much. Don't even need the sling anymore. Everybody's making a bigger deal of this than it is."

"Aunt Mila, Mommy said you got two boo boos. Did the doctor give you medicine?"

Camilla knelt down so she was eye level with Jamie, and Heath thought it was the sweetest thing he'd ever seen. She had such a caring heart, and he only hoped there'd be enough room for him in there someday.

"Yep, the doctors gave me medicine and I'm all better. But they didn't give me the good Band-Aids with superheroes on them. I got the plain ones, even though I asked nicely." A pretend frown pursed her lips and Heath bit back a chuckle.

Jamie's little hand reached forward and touched the white square taped to Camilla's forehead. "I got some mermaid ones at home. I can bring you one, if you want."

"Thank you, but I get to take this one off tomorrow, and won't need a new one. We'll save it for next time, okay?"

Better not be a next time.

"Alright, everybody inside," Ms. Patti's affectionate yet firm tone had the assembled crowd heading indoors. "No sense standing on the porch gabbing. Let poor Camilla and Heath catch their breath."

Heath's eyes met his father's, who gave him a knowing look and a single nod. He wondered if Uncle Gator called him. Probably. There wasn't much they kept from each other, not when it came to family.

As he walked past, his father murmured, "We'll talk later."

That was code for his father wanting answers, and Heath knew he wouldn't take no for an answer.

"Rafe and Tessa will be by later. I know he wants to talk with you." His momma patted his cheek and strode past him into the kitchen. From his place just outside the kitchen, his eyes met Camilla's, hers round at being the center of attention. Probably not someplace she occupied often. He'd noted on her previous visits she tended to fade into the background. Whether it was a deliberate thing, or something she did subconsciously, he wasn't sure. She'd soon learn being around the Boudreaus, nobody stayed out of the spotlight forever, especially when they had a bull's-eye painted on their back.

He knew his brothers would demand answers, along with helping come up with a game plan for keeping Camilla safe while she was in Shiloh Springs. Brody and his father stood off to the side, watching closely as Beth and Jamie peppered Camilla with a million questions she gamely answered.

His mother handed him a glass of sweet tea, stood on her tiptoes and waited for him to lean down, before pressing a kiss against his cheek. Because she was height deprived, he always teased her about needing a ladder to give him a hug. One year, for Christmas, he'd bought her a plastic stepstool, claiming he was getting a crick in his neck from bending over all the time.

"What did the doctors say?" His momma leaned against his side, her eyes studying Camilla. "Do we need to take her in to see Doc Jennings?"

"She's fine. They checked her thoroughly at the hospital in North Carolina. She's taking her antibiotics and has some pain medications, though she hasn't needed to take any recently."

"We'll take good care of her, until you figure out who's trying to hurt her." She put a hand on his arm and squeezed. "Then we'll take care of them." The bloodthirsty smile she shot him would have chilled the blood of anybody who didn't know her. Heath merely nodded once and turned his attention back to Camilla.

"Yes, ma'am."

Heath heard the front door open behind him and glanced over his shoulder, spotting Rafe and his fiancé, Tessa. Her hair was mussed, and she was frantically smoothing it down, her cheeks flushed. From the smirk on his brother's face, he had a good idea what they'd been up to.

"Trip go okay?"

Heath nodded to his brother, watching as Tessa hugged Camilla, and grabbed the chair beside her, jumping headlong into the ongoing conversation. "Had to leave New Orleans sooner than I'd planned. I screwed up."

"What happened?"

"I forgot to take Camilla's phone away. I had a burner to give her, so she'd be able to keep in contact for her publishing stuff. Instead, I got wrapped up in my own head and didn't notice until it was too late. We went to dinner in the French Quarter. She'd never been, so we played tourist. She pulled out her phone and started taking pictures. Fortunately, I did remember to have her power it down before that, so it was only on for a short time, but…"

"Anybody with computer skills could track the GPS." Rafe clapped him on the back. "Don't feel bad, we all screw up sometimes. Not the first time, probably won't be the last. Just means we keep our eyes open."

"I've got her phone now, and she's got the burner. Ridge

said his computer guru, Destiny, could go through it, see if anything looks suspicious. She's also going to see if any spyware has been installed."

"Wouldn't Camilla know if somebody loaded something on her phone?"

Heath shook his head. "I did some reading about it. Somebody could send a text or an e-mail with a photo attached. As soon as it's clicked on, the app is downloaded onto the phone without the user ever knowing."

Rafe sighed and leaned against the doorjamb. "Sometimes I hate technology. Just when you think you've got a handle on things, they come up with a couple dozen new programs to screw up your life."

"Yep, it's a blessing and a curse."

"Do you think you caught a tail in New Orleans?"

"Don't think so. Uncle Gator borrowed one of Carpenter Security Services cars, so it's clean. No way to trace it back to him or me. Not unless they go through a mountain of holding companies and subsidiaries. He took off for North Carolina sometime after midnight. He's going to talk to Officer Dandridge, then do a little digging on his on."

"Wow, that's like Camilla getting the family seal of approval."

Heath's grin spoke far more than words. Camilla might not understand, but he knew the rest of the family would. She'd already been accepted by his parents, and that cinched things as far as he was concerned. Having his uncle accept her, go out of his way to assist in figuring out who was gunning for her, was like the cherry on top of the sundae.

A movement from across the kitchen caught his eye, and his father move toward the back door, giving a single jerk of his head. With a quick glance at Camilla, who was still surrounded by all the womenfolk, he surreptitiously made his way across the kitchen and eased out the door, following his father to the barn.

Time to make plans to keep the woman he loved safe.

CHAPTER TEN

C amilla followed Beth to the front porch and settled onto the big swing. Covered with a thick cushion and lots of pillows along the back, she snuggled into the softness and sighed. Her muscles slowly unclenched, partly from the long car ride, and partly from tension she'd been carrying since leaving New Orleans. Being around the Boudreaus, Beth, and Jamie, she felt safe enough to let her guard down.

The gentle back and forth movement of the swing was almost hypnotic, the barely there squeak from the chains holding it up a soothing lullaby. The silence stretched for almost a full minute, then two. She wondered how long it would take for Beth to finally explode with questions. Biting her bottom lip to hold back a chuckle, she started counting. When she hit five, Beth swiveled on the swing, facing her.

"Are you really okay? You're not lying to keep me from worrying?"

"I swear on a stack of my books, I am not lying. I'm fine. My arm barely hurts. It twinges a bit if I move too fast without thinking. I didn't even put a bandage on it today after my shower. The one on my forehead comes off tomorrow."

Beth grabbed her hand, squeezing tight. "I was so scared, Camilla. When I got the call from the hospital saying you were in the emergency room unconscious and you'd been shot, I lost it. Brody's my rock, and I love him to pieces, but I was ready to drop everything, race straight to the airport, and catch the next flight to Charlotte."

"Well, I'm glad he talked some sense into you."

Beth shook her head. "He didn't. I think he'd have been right beside me on the plane. Heath's the one who took charge. He started making calls, reservations, everything. Got me calmed down. Told me he'd take care of you." Leaning her head against Camilla's shoulder, she whispered, "He cares about you. More than he's willing to admit."

Shock rolled through Camilla as she contemplated Beth's words. She couldn't be right. He'd been sweet and kind. Funny. Sensitive to her needs. Could it be something more?

"He's taken good care of me, I'll give you that much. He took charge immediately. Kind of rolled over me like a steamroller, but he got things done."

Beth giggled, the sound infectious. "A typical Boudreau male. They can't stand to see a woman in peril. It's the whole damsel-in-distress thing. These men learned it by example. Nobody can ever accuse Douglas Boudreau of standing on the sidelines when a woman or child is in trouble. Look what he did when Jamie was kidnapped."

"They're all larger than life. More like the men I write

about, but never seem to find in real life." Camilla started the swing moving again, her toes against the porch, the subtle movement soothing her deep inside. "Heath overwhelms me sometimes. I'm afraid…"

"He'd never hurt you!"

Camilla gave Beth an exasperated look. "Not that kind of afraid. I'm worried if I open myself up to him, it'll make me vulnerable. He overwhelms me, you know? Not in a bad way, because I know he'd never hurt me. It's—if I let myself, I could fall in love with him."

"What's wrong with that? He's a good man, one of the best besides my Brody. Strong. Compassionate. Loves his family and his friends. I know he flirts a lot, but personally I think that's a defense mechanism. It keeps him from letting anybody get too close."

"He doesn't really flirt with me. Oh, there're subtle little things, but nothing like I've seen him do with others." Camilla's protest was barely above a whisper.

Beth leaned back and met Camilla's gaze. "Seriously?"

She nodded. "Don't get me wrong. He's attentive and pays attention when I talk. He tells me I'm beautiful. On the plane ride to New Orleans, it felt like we were the only two people in the world. It was magical. But I wouldn't really call that flirting, right? Unless you count the endless times he's tormented me. Like the first time I visited here and he swiped my laptop." Her lips curved at the memory, though at the time she'd wanted to rip his head off.

"Don't you find it telling, that his attentions are casual with other women, but with you..."

"With me what?"

Beth rolled her eyes. "Hello? Ms. Romance Writer, are you being deliberate obtuse? He likes you. He *really* likes you. Shoot, he's probably halfway in love with you."

Camilla's eyes widened at Beth's statement. "I think you're reading far too much into this."

"And I think you're being deliberately ignorant. For somebody so smart, you are oblivious to what's right in front of you." Beth shrugged. I'm just saying. I'll stop pushing—for now."

"Good. Because you're so far out in left field, sister, you're practically outside the ballpark."

"We'll see. Anyway, I meant to ask earlier. Do you still not remember anything about the shooting?"

Camilla wrapped her arms across her middle, a shiver running down her spine. "Nothing. No matter how hard I try, there's nothing there. From Saturday night after I left my parents' house, until I woke up in the emergency room is a total blank."

"I'm sorry. I can't imagine having a chunk of my memories missing."

"The doctors said I might get bits and pieces, or I may never remember at all. It's called retrograde amnesia. Nothing else is missing. It's driving me crazy, because I know stuff happened and I don't have a clue."

"I wish there was something you could try to jog the memories loose. Like hypnosis or regression therapy."

Before Camilla could answer, another car pulled up the driveway, a silver hybrid, and screeched to a stop. Nica bounded from the driver's side, sprinting toward the porch, her long blonde hair pulled high in a ponytail. She was clad in jeans washed to almost white, with holes in the knees that were from wear and not from a designer label. She bounded toward the swing, plopping herself down between Camilla and Beth with a grin. She did a little judicious wiggling to fit between them, and then she flung her arms around their shoulders.

"Am I late? Did I miss all the juicy details?"

Camilla looked at Beth and burst into laughter while Nica smiled. Beth wiped tears from her eyes before winking at Camilla.

"You didn't miss anything. Your father and brothers are being their normal, gallant, overprotective selves. Your Uncle Gator has gone to North Carolina to figure out who's trying to hurt Camilla. And Heath's trying to act all cool and manly, but he can't keep his eyes off Camilla."

"Beth—"

"What? It's the truth. He watches you like you're a juicy T-bone steak and he hasn't eaten in days."

Nica leaned back and sighed. "Man, I love this family." She used her foot to propel the swing back, starting the softly swaying motion again. "When Momma called, I dropped everything and headed here." She reached up and gently touched the bandage on Camilla's forehead.

"Really, I'm fine. Doctor gave me a clean bill of health. I need to finish my antibiotics, but other than that, I'm good."

Nica's gaze hardened. "Except somebody shot you. Let's not forget that."

"It's kinda hard to forget. Of course, it's not like I can remember it happening."

"I heard you have retrograde amnesia. That stinks."

"We were talking about that when you came roaring up the drive." Beth grinned when Nica stuck out her tongue. "I asked Camilla if she'd considered getting hypnosis or something like that."

"Might not be a bad idea." Nica eyed her up and down, and Camilla wondered if this was what a bug felt like under a microscope. "Have you considered meditation? We covered it in one of my classes."

"Meditation? Like in yoga?"

Nica rolled her eyes at Beth's question. "There's more to meditation than yoga. Some meditation can be used as a type of self-hypnosis. Others work with regression or trying to delve into your past lives. What I'm suggesting is simply sitting quietly, letting everything around you fade, and allowing your mind to relax. No specific focusing on pinpointing a specific event, or worrying about why you can't remember."

Camilla let Nica's words roll around in her brain and

couldn't come up with an argument for not giving it a shot. What was the worst that could happen?

"I'm game. What do I need to do to get ready?"

Nica chuckled. "First off, we need to get Heath out of the house, preferably off the ranch. He means well, but I can't see him sitting idly by while you tried meditating. No offense, but my big brother can be a pain in the butt, especially when he's trying to help."

"He's not that bad," Camilla protested.

"Really? You're telling me he hasn't steamrollered over everybody and everything to keep you out of the line of fire since the minute he landed in Charlotte? He didn't deal with the hospital, or the local police, or getting you here?"

Camilla didn't argue—she couldn't. Because he'd done exactly what Nica accused.

"Alright, we send Heath into town for something. We'll figure it out. Now, when would you like to do it?" Nica climbed from the swing and turned to face her.

"As soon as possible. If I can remember something— anything—maybe I can get my life back. Because I'm sick of being scared all the time." She pointed her finger at Nica. "Don't you dare tell your brother I said that. He's practically my shadow now. If he thinks I'm afraid, he'll be attached to my hip and I'll never have any privacy. And, personally, I like going to the bathroom by myself."

Nica and Beth laughed until tears ran down their cheeks, and Nica held out her hand, pulling Camilla off the swing.

"Come on, let's grab Momma. She'll get Heath and the rest of the men out of the house before you can say boo."

Still laughing, they headed into the house.

"Have you found her?"

"Not yet," the gravelly voice on the other end of the phone replied. "I followed her phone's GPS to right outside the French Quarter in New Orleans. Unfortunately, her phone hasn't been turned on since that last signal."

"What's she doing in New Orleans?"

"No clue. I searched her place thoroughly and found nothing. Her computer is gone. Looked like she left in a hurry. I trashed the place, took some stuff to make it look like a robbery. Which is exactly what the police report will show."

"What about the man who showed up at the hospital? What have you been able to find out about him?" Anger simmered beneath the surface when he thought about Camilla Stewart. The wretched woman had been in the wrong place at the wrong time, and now she could ruin him. Destroy everything he'd carefully worked for. He couldn't let that happen.

"I've got my people working up a profile on him. His name is Heath Boudreau, at least that's the name he gave at the hospital. Flashed an ATF badge."

He straightened at that revelation. "He works for the government?"

"If it's a true credential. Might be as real as the ones I flash when I need information. A good one can be faked for about fifty bucks."

The squeezing pain in his chest eased a little. "Boudreau? The name's not familiar. Should I be concerned?"

"Don't know. I'll know more by this evening. He seems intuitive if he's the one who's keeping her off the phone. And looks like he's got friends in New Orleans, because there's no hotel records under his name or Camilla Stewart. Unless they're camping in the bayou, or going incognito, they're staying with somebody."

"Any other Boudreaus in New Orleans?"

There was a long pause before the other man answered. "It's a common name here apparently. A couple of different spellings, but it's like Smith or Jones. It'll take a while to see if there's a familial connection, but I'm assuming we'll find one."

Closing his eyes, he drew in a deep breath, trying to contain his rage. "Find them. Take him out if you have to, but bring Camilla Stewart to me."

CHAPTER ELEVEN

C amilla allowed herself to be pulled into Nica's bedroom, with Beth bringing up the rear. She wasn't sure how she felt about Nica's idea of meditation to try and recover her memories, but at this point she was willing to try anything. Having a continual blank place when she *knew* something happened and having no clue what was disconcerting. An itch she couldn't scratch, an irritation that picked at her subconscious, and she didn't want to admit it was driving her crazy.

"Okay, let's make you comfortable. You want to sit on the bed or the floor?"

"Floor, I think. It's what I always see people doing yoga do, right?"

"Forget everything you've ever heard about meditation or self-hypnosis or anything else. No preconceived notions. You're simply going to relax and clear your mind. It's simple."

"Darn. I was hoping it would be like the movies. She'd close her eyes and boom, all her memories would come flooding back." Beth did a dramatic gesture and fell back on the floor, laughing hilariously. Camilla grabbed a pillow and whacked her upside the head with it. Nica giggled and plopped on the floor beside her.

"Don't stress about it. If you remember anything, it's good. If you don't, it's good, too. We're simply going to relax. Deep breaths. No pressure."

"I'm not a very relaxed person," Camilla whispered. "I live with deadlines and high pressure most of the time. Chances are good this won't work."

Nica shook her head and pointed a finger at her. "This is a no negativity zone. Only positive energy allowed." Her expression was so like her mother's, Camilla felt the corners of her mouth turning up.

"Yes, ma'am."

Beth's face was in her hands, and her whole body rocked with laughter. Her shoulders shook and she made little gasping sounds, developing into giggles. Nica gave her a backhanded pop on the arm to get her attention, and Beth sucked in air, her laughter fading with each breath.

"Sorry, sorry. I'll be good, I promise."

"This isn't going to work if you can't stop laughing. Camilla needs quiet and serenity. Think you can manage that, Chuckles?"

Beth nodded vigorously, both hands slapped against her mouth.

"Alright, let's start. Cam, you comfortable?"

Camilla's body jerked at Nica's use of the nickname.

"You called me Cam."

Nica's eyes widened at her words. "It's what Heath calls you. I guess I've started thinking of you by that name. I can call you Camilla if it bothers you."

"No, it's okay. I've never had a nickname, not really. Jamie calls me Aunt Milla. Nobody but Heath ever calls me Cam." She blushed. "I kind of like it."

"Alrighty." Nica and Beth grinned. "Cam it is. Now, are you comfortable? Want a cushion or pillow to sit on?

"I'm good. What's next?"

"Relax. Close your eyes and take a deep breath. Hold it for a few seconds. Slowly blow it out. Good. Do it again."

Camilla listened to Nica's voice. She talked softly, her voice calm and sweet, her soft Texas twang sounding right somehow. It reminded her of Ms. Patti's kindness and welcome. Shoot, if she was honest, it sounded like home.

Keeping her eyes closed, she continued taking deep breaths, and tried to wipe away everything, concentrating on keeping her feeling of contentment and peacefulness centered inside her. She wasn't sure how much time passed, with neither Nica nor Beth saying a word. Maybe knowing they were there beside her, doing their best to help her recover her memories, made her feel all warm and tingly.

"Cam, think about the day of your missing memories. What is the last thing you remember?"

She focused her thoughts on trying to remember the last few moments she recalled. Saturday night. Dinner with her parents. Getting home, still irritated with her parents' bullheaded stubbornness in supporting Evan's idiocy. Frustrated they refused to admit their son wasn't the man he'd pretended to be; instead he'd been a monster filled with greed, capable of murder.

"I came home Saturday night after dinner with my folks. Not a happy meal."

She heard Beth's snicker, but pushed it out, needing to concentrate. This was important. The memories tickled at the back of her mind, tantalizingly close enough she could almost reach out and touch them.

"I brushed my teeth and went to bed."

"Keep going," Nica encouraged, her voice soft.

"I got up the next morning and made coffee." Camilla took another deep breath, imagining the unmistakable scent of freshly brewed coffee. "I remember I used the last of the coffee, and knew I had to pick up some at the grocery." Huh, that was new. She hadn't remembered that until now. Another deep breath, slowly released. "I did my usual routine. E-mails, answering calls. Posting things on social media. Then I worked.

"You're doing amazingly well, Cam. Let's go a little farther. You wrote for a while. What happened after that?"

Camilla struggled to move forward. Like slogging through the mud on a riverbank, like when she'd been younger. She'd sink deep, past her ankles and cried for Evan to help her before she disappeared beneath the mud. He'd laughed and walked away, leaving her to her own devices. Each step had been an almost impossible task, but she'd fought the brackish mud threatening to swallow her. Made her way to safety.

"I…I don't know. It's black." She heard the thread of fear in her voice, felt the vicelike grip in her chest. Her breath caught in her throat, the edges of blackness edging closer behind her eyelids.

"Alright, Cam. Everything is fine. You're in your home and you're safe. Take a deep breath."

"Maybe we should stop." Another voice added, and Camilla recognized it as Beth's. She didn't want to stop. Something important was right beyond her grip, and if she could reach out and grasp it, maybe she'd have the answers she needed.

"Cam, focus on what's around you. Can you hear anything? Feel anything? You've got senses beyond sight—use them. Focus on your surroundings. Slow and easy."

"I can hear the TV. I keep it on when I'm writing; it's kind of a white noise in the background, so that it's not total silence." Reaching up, she rubbed her forehead, which was scrunched up. "I think, no, I'm sure, I hear a dog barking outside. Sounded like it was in distress."

"Good. Did you go outside?"

"Yes! I remember saving my work and going out to check on the dog. I…darn it, come on! I can't—I can't remember anything else." Camilla opened her eyes, and rubbed her eyes with the heels of her hands. "That's it. There's nothing after that.

Beth scooted over beside her and wrapped her arms around Camilla. "You did awesome!

Camilla glanced at Nica, whose grin held a hint of a satisfied smirk. "How much of that was new information?"

"Quite a bit actually. Before, I'd only remembered up to leaving my parents' house on Saturday night. I didn't remember getting home or anything else. Now, I've remembered Sunday morning's events. I wondered why I went outside. A dog barking, sounding like it was in distress? Definitely would have had me heading outdoors."

Nica stood and held out her hand, helping Camilla up. Beth clamored to her feet. Impulsively, Camilla hugged Nica. Excitement bubbled inside her. At least she'd accomplished something with Nica's experiment. It was a start. The doctors said her memories might start returning. After this, she at least had hope they were right.

Nica opened her bedroom door and stepped into the hall. "I'm hungry. Let's head to the kitchen and see if those savages left any cookies."

The next morning, Heath headed to Gracie's place. Figured he'd grab a decent cup of coffee before meeting up with Rafe. They'd decided after talking to their dad, if they laid out all the facts, made a detailed timeline from the point of Camilla's shooting forward, they'd come up with something or somebody to look closer at.

Standing in line, he glanced around at the customers, mostly people he'd known ever since he'd moved in with the Boudreaus. Good, hardworking, God-fearing people who loved the town of Shiloh Springs as much as he did. He smiled at Dante Monroe, who stood at the front of the line. Rafe mentioned Lucas took Dante under his wing, especially after the investigative article where Dante played a huge part. The younger man was thriving with the attention, as well as holding down a job with Frank at the garage.

"Afternoon, Heath. Jill mentioned you were visiting. Glad to see you." Dante held two large cups in his hands, a ready smile on his face.

"How's your sister?"

"Happier than I've ever seen her. She's over the moon in love with Lucas, and he's gaga over her. The bakery's doing fabulous, too."

"Glad to hear it. I'll have to stop by while I'm here."

"Do that. I know she'll be thrilled to see you. I've gotta run, Frank gets cranky if he doesn't get his caffeine." Dante chuckled. "He used to drink that swill he made in the office pot. I started bringing him the good stuff, and now he's spoiled."

"Frank's a good guy. A little spoiling won't hurt him."

He watched Dante head out the door and moved a couple steps forward in the line. The smell of the coffee permeated the air, and he drew in a deep breath. He spotted Gracie behind the register, her dark hair highlighting the high cheekbones and ready smile he'd come to know. She was a sweetheart, and at one point he'd considered dating her. Too bad she'd been interested in somebody else. Of course, now he didn't regret a thing, because he'd found the woman of his dreams in a feisty package, and she was sitting at the Big House, waiting for his return.

"Heath! Welcome home!"

"Hey, Gracie. How could I stay away from the best coffee west of the Mississippi?" He studied her closely. Took in the shadows beneath her eyes, and the slight pallor to her skin. It wasn't obvious at first, unless you were looking closely, and a wave of concern swept through him. "Everything alright?"

She started, her shoulders tensing, and then she pasted a smile on her lips and gave him a wink. "Look around, big guy. Things are great. I've got enough business I've had to hire extra staff."

"You know you can call me if you need anything, right?"

She drew in a deep breath and slowly exhaled before meeting his eyes directly. "I know, hon. Now, what can I get you?"

He placed an order for a large coffee and took it over to a bistro-style table by the window. From here, he could people watch as familiar folks strolled down Main Street. Taking a sip, he savored the dark roast with its tang of bitterness. Perfect.

When his cell rang, he didn't bother looking at the caller ID, simply answered.

"Heath, I heard you were in town. How're you doing, son?"

Heath was surprised to hear Doc Jennings' voice. He hadn't talked to the older man in months. "Doc. Nice to hear your voice. It's been a while."

"Sure has. You still up in D.C. working with the ATF?"

"Yes, sir."

"Bet your momma and dad are glad to have you home. Especially with everything going on."

Heath straightened in his chair, every instinct going into red alert. What was Doc Jennings talking about? He couldn't possibly know about Camilla; nobody outside the family did. Of course, most of his focus had been on Camilla and trying to figure out her shooting. Had he missed something else happening in his own backyard?

"Doc, I've been out of the loop. What are you talking about?"

There was a long moment before he heard a sigh. "Son of a gun, I should've kept my flapping jaws shut."

"Too late, Doc. Spill it." Heath's hand tightened around his cup, an eerie sense of foreboding swamping him. Whatever Doc told him, it wouldn't be good, and he knew deep in his gut it involved one of his brothers. Somebody was in for a world of hurt, because nobody messed with his family. Boudreaus looked out for each other.

"It's about Rafe."

Dang, he hated being right. "What about him?"

"I was approached a couple of weeks ago to sign some load of crapola-on-a-cracker petition to yank Rafe from his rightful place as sheriff. Of course, I told them to stick their clipboard where the sun don't shine. Idiots, the whole lot of 'em."

"Hold up. I want to make sure I'm hearing you right. Somebody is circulating a petition to have Rafe removed as sheriff?"

"Yep. Weren't many signatures on the one I saw, so that's good news." Doc's voice lowered. "You ask me, somebody's got a stick up their backside. Probably somebody who's had a run-in with your brother and came out on the short end of the deal. I've known all of you boys since you were knee high, and whoever's doing this is out of their mind. Like I said, bunch of idiots."

"Anybody else know about this petition?" Heath could feel the rage building inside, a slow burn that if left unchecked would spill over into everything, until he exploded in a ball of anger and violence. He hadn't felt like this in a long time. Exercise and focused breathing usually helped, but he had the feeling the only thing that might alleviate his growing wrath would be getting to the bottom of who'd gone after his brother.

"Wish I could help, but I don't have a clue. The woman soliciting signatures was somebody I didn't recognize. Not one of my patients, that's for sure. I could ask around, but honestly, I don't want to draw any attention to this nonsense."

A horrible thought hit Heath like a sledgehammer. "Do my parents know about this petition?"

"Heck, no. Not that I now about anyway. I expect if I did, I'd be patching up whoever is behind the worthless piece of paper."

Heath hissed as hot coffee spilled across his hand. He hadn't realized he'd squeezed his cup hard enough for the lid to pop off. Grabbing napkins, he mopped up the mess and stood, tossing everything into the trash.

"Thanks, Doc. I appreciate you telling me about this. I'm gonna nip this in the bud. Now, if you'll excuse me, I think I need to talk to my big brother, and find out why he's kept this to himself."

Doc chuckled. "I'll keep the office open late, in case either of you need stitches."

Heath gave a broken laugh, the sound low and deep. Wouldn't be the first time he or one of his brothers ended up at the clinic getting patched up after one of their tussles.

"Talk with you soon, Doc."

Hanging up, he waved to Gracie and left, his long strides eating up the distance as he headed toward the sheriff's office.

Time to talk to Rafe.

CHAPTER TWELVE

H eath flung the door to the sheriff's office open wide and stomped inside, stopping short when he spotted Sally Anne in the middle of the hallway leading to his brother's office. He pulled up, noting the startled look on her face, and took a deep breath. It wasn't right to take his aggravation out on her. Nope, he needed to direct it at the person who deserved it—his brother. Heck, she was an innocent bystander, and he wouldn't let her become collateral damage, though the rage coursing through his bloodstream kept his temper on a razor's edge.

"Afternoon, Sally Anne. You doing okay?"

"Well, well, Heath Boudreau. You're a sight for sore eyes, but you seem a bit riled up. Anything I can help with?"

He had no difficulty reading her anxiety tinged with compassion, and her expression softened as she took a step forward, placing a hand on his arm. As far as he was concerned, Sally Anne was a saint for putting up with his brother, not to mention the rest of the Boudreau clan over the years. Even though she tended toward gossip more than most, both listening and spreading, she had a kind and loving heart, so it was easy to forgive her for that slight transgression.

"Looking for the sheriff. He around?"

She smiled and pointed with her thumb over her shoulder. "He's in his office, working on some paperwork. Bet he could use a break."

"Excellent. Do me a favor. If you hear anything…unusual…coming from Rafe's office, ignore it."

Her penciled-on brows rose high on her forehead at his request, and she nodded. "Got it. Want some coffee before you head back?"

"No, thanks, I'm good. Just need to straighten out a few things with my brother."

"Alright. Give a shout if you change your mind." Reaching up, she patted his cheek. "You're a good boy, Heath. Glad to see you sticking around for more than one of your fly-by visits."

"I miss seeing your smiling face too, Sally Anne. How about we go to lunch soon? You can catch me up on everything I've missed."

"Sounds like a plan, hon. Now, you head on back and see your brother." Giving him an exaggerated wink, she walked past him to her desk, and put on her phone headset.

Heath took a deep breath and blew it out slowly before heading down the hall to Rafe's office. His brother better have some pretty darned good answers to his questions, or there'd be a big ole family "come to Jesus" meeting.

Not bothering to knock, he flung open the office door, hard enough it slammed against the wall with a loud bang. Rafe shot out of his chair like he'd been stuck with a cattle prod and stared at Heath.

"What's wrong?"

Heath stormed across the room, drew his fist back, and clocked his brother square in the nose. Blood spurted onto Rafe's shirtfront right before his backside hit the floor.

"Why didn't you tell me?" Heath's deep voice echoed through the office, and he stood with his hands on his hips, staring down at his brother, ineffectually swiping at the blood pouring from his nose.

"Sheriff?" Sally Anne's voice sounded down the hall, and Heath shook his head. He should have known she wouldn't be able to ignore what she'd heard. "You need me to call anybody?"

"Everything's fine." Heath knew his voice carried down the hall to the front desk. "We're working out a few issues. Family business."

By now, Rafe had struggled to his feet, a wadded-up napkin pressed to his bleeding nose. The glare he shot Heath would have had a lesser man quaking in his cowboy boots, but Heath wasn't about to let his brother intimidate him or avoid answering his questions. Not with something this important.

"What is wrong with you? You can't come in here throwing punches! Are you out of your mind?" Rafe tossed the napkin into the trash and glared at him. Heath drew himself up, towering over his brother, ready to throw another punch if he had to. It felt good to clock Rafe, though he'd pulled the punch at the last second, because he didn't really want to hurt him. Popping him a good one got his attention, and now he planned to get some long-overdue answers.

"Might ask you the same thing, bro. Want to tell me about the petition circulating around Shiloh Springs? The one you haven't bothered to mention to anyone in the family?"

The color leeched from Rafe's face, and Heath knew he'd scored a direct hit. His shoulders slumped as he moved back behind his desk and slid onto his chair. "How'd you find out?"

"Does it matter? I want to know what you're doing about it."

Rafe sighed and touched his nose, grimacing. "Did you have to hit so hard? You could have just asked me."

"Nope, you'd have tap-danced around the issue and never answered my question. I'm still waiting for an answer, by the way, and I'm not leaving until I get a satisfactory one. Of course, I could always call Dad. Bet you wouldn't try to skirt around answering him."

"Don't do that!" Rafe's voice got louder with each word. Then he physically seemed to deflate. "Bro, there's not a whole lot to tell you. The petition's been circulating around the county for a few weeks. If they can get ten percent of the registered voters to sign, it can be submitted, asking for my removal."

"So, let me get this straight, because I want to make sure I have all the facts right before I beat the living snot out of you." Heath plopped down in the chair on the other side of Rafe's desk, and stared at his brother. "You've known about this recall petition for weeks and you haven't told anybody."

"Lucas knows. He found out and confronted me." Rafe shot Heath a dirty look. "Of course, he didn't hit me. I told him the same thing I'm telling you. Stay out of it. If the people of this county lack confidence in me, think I'm not doing my job properly, they've got the right to kick me out of office and elect somebody else to do the job."

"Horsepucky!" Heath shot back with one of his colorful curses. "It's not like you to simply lie down and die. You're a Boudreau. Man up." He studied Rafe closely, noting his brother wouldn't meet his gaze. "Any idea who the jackass is behind this idiotic campaign to get a new sheriff? No, wait, let me guess. The Calloways?"

Rafe gave a halfhearted nod. "That's my suspicion, although I don't have any official confirmation they're behind this."

"I understand why you didn't tell me. I live halfway across the country, though I'm thoroughly pissed you've kept something like this to yourself. Dude, I'm shocked nobody else in the family's heard about this. You've gotta know it's bound to come out, and I can't see Momma sitting by idly wringing her hands, can you?" Heath pantomimed the motion and they both laughed.

"Honestly, bro, how'd you hear about it?"

"Doc Jennings called me; said he'd heard I was in town for a visit. Mentioned he'd been approached to sign what he called and I quote, 'some load of crapola-on-a-cracker petition to yank you from your rightful place,' unquote." Heath folded his arms over his chest. "Of course, he told them to stick their clipboard where the sun don't shine. Now, imagine my surprise when I heard that little tidbit about my brother possibly losing his job."

"Well, crud. If Doc Jennings is spreading the word, it's probably gonna be all over town by nightfall."

Heath bared his teeth in a not-so-pleasant smile. "Guess you'd better get out to the Big House and tell the folks, before they hear it from somebody else, shouldn't ya?" He stood. "You know I've got your back, bro. Whatever you need, it's yours, just say the word."

Rafe stood, walked around the desk and hugged Heath. "I know, and I appreciate it. I've been sticking my head in the sand, hoping it would go way. Guess that's not gonna happen."

"They want a fight, they've got one. Nobody messes with a Boudreau, not unless they want a butt kicking they won't ever forget. Call the folks, or better yet, ride back to the Big House with me. I'm headed there now. Gotta see what kind of trouble Camilla's gotten into while I've been in town."

Rafe laughed and slapped Heath on the back. "Thanks. Think I'll take you up on that. I'll give Tessa a call, have her meet us there. She's not gonna be happy I kept this from her."

"Trust me, brother, she's not the only one who's gonna tear you a new one. I can't wait until Momma hears." Heath's booming laugh filled the room. "I'm going to say goodbye to Sally Anne. Meet me out front when you're ready."

"I'd better go wash my face first and change my shirt. Don't need any of the town folk to see their sheriff with a bloody nose." Rafe reached up and gingerly touched his nose. "Next time, don't hit so hard, dude."

"I ain't apologizing. You deserved it."

Rafe shot him his happy middle finger and walked out of the office. Heath headed toward the front, feeling a weight lift off his shoulders. He couldn't imagine the stress his brother had been dealing with, keeping something so important hidden from all the people who loved him. Yes, it was stupid, but a part of him understood Rafe's motive. Not the way he'd have handled things, but Heath was a fighter, not a lover or a peacemaker. And it had felt bloody good to land a solid punch on big brother's kisser. Reminded him of the good old days, when they'd been rowdy teenagers, causing their parents all kinds of grief. There'd been their fair share of bloody noses and bruises amongst all the Boudreau boys back then.

"Sally Anne, I'm stealing Rafe away for a bit."

She studied him intently, her steely-eyed gaze sharp behind her black-rimmed cat's eye glasses before a huge smile spread across her face.

"Hope you didn't hurt him too much with that punch." She stood and walked around her desk, perching her generous backside on the edge. "I suspect you heard what's been going on around here the last couple of weeks."

"You knew?" Rafe's voice was laced with surprise as he walked up to stand beside Heath. "You never said a word."

Sally Anne shrugged. "I figured you'd tell me when you were ready." She reached up and patted Rafe's cheek the way she had Heath's earlier. "By the way, I haven't told a soul. My word of honor, nobody's heard about it from me." She made a cross motion over her chest. "And let me tell you, it's been murder keeping this secret."

"You're a good woman, Sally Anne. Thank you." Rafe leaned down and kissed her cheek. "We're headed to the Big House, to let my folks know."

"About time." Her gaze flitted from Rafe to Heath and back again. "Last I heard," she whispered, "whoever started this petition ain't got a leg to stand on. When they tried to get me to sign, the page only had thirteen signatures on it. Thirteen! Most of 'em names I didn't recognize, so I'd say you ain't got anything to worry about."

Heath chuckled and slapped Rafe on the back. "Thirteen people isn't anywhere close to what they need. Shiloh

Springs might be small, but those numbers wouldn't even cause a ripple."

"Keep in mind, Sally Anne probably only saw one person's petition. They'll have more than one person trying to gather signatures."

"Nuh-uh." Sally Anne's grin spread across her face. "When I asked about the number of signatures, I was told they'd barely gotten anybody to sign, though not for the lack of trying."

"This is good news, my brother. Maybe we can keep Momma from going ballistic and grabbing her shotgun. I think she'd enjoy peppering the backsides of a couple of folks we know." Heath slapped Rafe on the back and saw his brother stumble from the unexpected gesture.

"Might as well get it over with. Can't avoid telling them any longer. Sally Anne, thank you for keeping this information to yourself. And I appreciate your show of support."

"You're a good boss, Sheriff Boudreau. Anybody who thinks differently will answer to me."

Heath turned and held open the front door, waiting for Rafe to exit. Before he'd made it more than two steps, Joel McAllister barreled through and skidded to a stop. He held up a hand and bent over, putting both hands on his knees, trying to catch his breath.

"Sheriff, we got a problem at the high school. Two guys...with guns...holding Mrs. Abernathy and her class..."

"Slow down, Joel." Rafe's gaze shot to Heath, who nodded. He read his brother loud and clear: they'd be headed for the high school instead of the Big House.

The phone rang, and Sally Anne hustled around the desk and answered, speaking in a slow and calm manner. Her words were murmured, but Heath's attention remained focused solely on Joel McAllister.

"Do you know the guys, Joel? Are they students at the school?"

Joel shook his head. "I don't know who they are, though I did see them hanging around the parking lot earlier this morning. I kinda snuck out of class, just for a couple of minutes, and I saw them standing next to a dark blue pickup."

"Please tell me you're not high. If you've been smoking weed again—"

"I swear I haven't touched any in months, Sheriff! I got your message loud and clear last time you busted me. Nope, I went out to my car because I was going to give Rachel something. It's her birthday. But I forgot and left her present in the trunk. These dudes were looking around like maybe they were waiting for somebody, then headed for the front entrance. Something about them didn't feel right, so I kinda followed 'em."

"Sheriff," Sally Anne interrupted and pointed at the phone, "that was the high school. What Joel said is true. Principal's evacuating the campus, and he's giving the same info as Joel. Two young males with guns. He didn't get a good look at the weapons, but thinks they're 9mm."

"Sally Anne, call Dusty and Jeb, have them meet us at the school. Also call Brody and have the fire department head to the high school. EMTs, first responders, everybody. Activate the emergency drill." Rafe pointed his finger at Joel. "You stay here."

"But, Sheriff—"

"No buts, Joel. You are a witness, and we'll need to get an official statement. For now, I want you here, out of the line of fire."

Joel drew in a deep breath and nodded. "Make sure Rachel's okay. If anything happens to her—"

"Nothing's going to happen to Rachel or anybody else. Sally Anne, don't let him leave."

"You got it, Sheriff."

Without another word, Heath followed his brother out the door and climbed onto the front seat of Rafe's truck, and they rode in silence the short distance to the high school. Two sheriff's vehicles were already in the parking lot, and Heath heard approaching sirens, knew the fire department and EMTs wouldn't be far behind.

Heath watched a stream of students race across the parking lot, being directed by the principal and teachers past the rows of parked cars, and onto the sidewalk. They formed into several groups. Some of the girls cried, while others attempted to comfort them. So far, it didn't look like anybody was having hysterics, though he wasn't sure how long that'd last once the parents found out what was going on. Adding parents to the chaos would be like pouring gasoline on a bonfire.

"What do we know?" Rafe questioned Dusty as he jogged over to join them. "Has everyone been evacuated?"

"Jeb's checking the halls and classrooms for stragglers. Once he gives the all clear, the only ones that'll still be inside are the students in Mrs. Abernathy's class where the two gunmen are holed up. I checked around the side, trying to get a look into her classroom. The blinds have been closed on the windows, so there's no direct line of sight."

"What about the cameras?"

Jeb shook his head. "They don't have them in the classrooms, only in the halls and cafeteria area."

"Okay," Rafe motioned to Brody and Antonio, "I need you to head around to the back of the school. Check for egress or any entry or exit points. Keep your eyes open for anybody hanging around that shouldn't be back there. You see anybody, send them around to the parking lot. Anybody gives you grief, call us." He gestured toward himself and Heath. "We'll handle it."

"I'll handle it," Heath corrected his brother's statement. "Rafe's gonna be too busy getting people coordinated and trying to contact the men inside."

He smiled at Rafe's scowled, but noted his brother didn't contradict him. Wouldn't do any good, because he had too much on his plate as it was. He could handle a few stragglers.

After the day he'd had, he looked forward to busting a few heads.

Antonio raised his cell phone. "I've called Williamson, given him a head's up. He's on his way, and he's bringing a hostage negotiator with him. We were lucky; they were at lunch together. Should be here in less than an hour. In the meantime, keep trying to open the lines of communication."

"Sally Anne's getting me Mrs. Abernathy's cell phone number. Hopefully, she has it in her classroom."

Rafe's phone rang and he answered. After a short conversation, he hung up and took a deep breath.

"Got the number?" Heath asked the question, knowing the others wanted to know too.

"Yeah." He took a deep breath. "Y'all have your orders. Let's get those kids home."

CHAPTER THIRTEEN

Camilla raced into the Big House's kitchen at Ms. Patti's shout. She'd been sitting in the cozy, overstuffed chair in the living room, with her feet on an ottoman, her laptop on her lap, staring at the blank screen. The story she'd been working on before Heath dragged her to Texas was flat and uninteresting. If she was honest, it was boring. The words wouldn't flow, because she couldn't concentrate on anything except Heath. Ms. Patti's call was a more than welcome reprieve.

"I'm here."

"Good. I need your help." Ms. Patti had stacks of things piled onto the kitchen table. Loaves of bread, packages of cold cuts, lettuce and tomatoes, and several bags of chips and pretzels. "Would you mind fixing as many sandwiches as you can with what's there?"

"I can handle that." Reaching for the bread, she pulled all the slices free and stacked them into two piles, and began assembling the ham, cheese, lettuce and tomatoes, and wrapped each one individually with cling wrap. Ms. Patti moved swiftly from cabinet to pantry, pulling out packages of cookies and other snacks.

"Are you planning on feeding an army? This seems like an awful lot of food."

Ms. Patti paused in the middle of the floor and drew in a deep breath. "Sorry, I should have explained, but I wanted to get things moving. There's a situation in town at the high school. All of the county's first responders have been called in. I've been rallying the troops. We'll make sure there's plenty of food, coffee, water. Whatever they need."

"Sounds pretty serious. Is there anything more I can do than make sandwiches? I've taken a couple of first aid courses, and I'm certified in CPR."

Ms. Patti unloaded the stack of food in her arms, and patted Camilla's shoulder. "Hopefully it won't come to that. Sally Anne at the sheriff's office called, said there's a hostage situation at the high school. A couple of men barricaded themselves in one of the classrooms."

Camilla dropped the piece of bread she'd picked up. "Oh, no! That's horrible."

"The rest of the school's been evacuated. We're heading into town and setting up a couple of relief stations. Gracie's bringing in tons of coffee from her shop. Jill's bringing everything she's got already baked in the store and closing down for the day. Daisy's got the diner fixing soup and anything else she can, so people have a hot meal. The church ladies are gathering blankets, quilts, anything else they think might be needed."

Camilla began assembling more sandwiches, though her mind immediately went to Heath, praying he was safe. She knew he'd be at the high school, right in the thick of things, because that's the kind of man he was, putting others before himself.

"Sounds like you've got everything covered."

"When Rafe first took office, there was a complete revamping of the emergency response guidelines, making sure we have protocols in place for every contingency. Rafe had Sally Anne activate it as soon as the hostage situation started."

"I don't know, it seems surreal. We hear about these kinds of things happening, but it's always someplace else, you know? Different cities, people you don't know personally. I've only been here a short time, but I feel like I know so many people in Shiloh Springs. Part of my family lives here, because I consider Beth and Jamie family, regardless of everything that happened with my brother."

"I know Beth feels the same, and Jamie misses you like crazy. I'm sure they consider you family, too." Ms. Patti walked into the pantry, returning with a couple of empty cardboard boxes and a large cooler. "Looks like we've got quite a bit of food ready. Let's load these up and head to town. It's going to take a while to get there."

Camilla placed one of the boxes on the table, and began stacking the sandwiches inside. The other box was soon loaded with chips, cookies, and other snacks.

"This has to be killing you, Ms. Patti. All of your sons are involved in one way or another with jobs helping others, and putting themselves in the path of danger. I admire you. These are your children. I can't imagine the stress you go through every day."

"Honestly, there's not a day that goes by I don't worry about all my children. But what should I do, tell them not to do the jobs they love? All I can do is hope and pray they're protected and safe. I'm scared, but my boys were raised to be independent, compassionate men. I have to give them my support and my love, even when I'm scared to death."

Camilla stuck out her hand. "Keys."

"What?"

"Give me the keys. I'll drive. You get in the passenger side and make phone calls, coordinate, do what you do best. I can manage to get us to town."

Ms. Patti dropped the Escalade's keys into Camilla's hand. "Thank you. I'm so glad you're here."

"Me too."

The drive to downtown Shiloh Springs took close to an hour. Camilla followed the directions Ms. Patti gave, turning onto a side street off Main. After about a mile and a half, she ran into a jumble of cars, all jockeying toward the high school. Forward movement crawled like a snail. She'd probably make better time parking the car and walking than the snail's pace they'd managed.

"Stop the car." Ms. Patti's hand lightly tapped hers on

the steering wheel.

Camilla's foot touched the brake, and she put the car into park. Ms. Patti opened the door and stood on the runner, and Camilla wondered if she'd lost her mind. When Ms. Patti put her fingers to her mouth and let out an earsplitting whistle, she was convinced. At least until she saw Chance striding toward them, a grim expression on his face.

"Momma, Camilla. Rafe told me to keep an eye out for you. Take the next right, then turn down the alley between the houses on your left." He pointed toward a short elderly man standing at the end of the alley. "Frank closed the garage and came down to help with keeping all the gawkers away. A few people tried to detour through the alley, and he's chasing 'em out."

Pretty smart.

"He'll let you through. When you get to the end, make another right and park by the fire truck. We've got volunteers waiting to help you set up."

"Have you heard anything yet? I'm worried about those poor children."

Chance shook his head. "Not so far, Momma. Rafe and Heath are coordinating things onsite. All I know is nobody's hurt. There haven't been any demands from whoever's holding Mrs. Abernathy or the kids. Derrick Williamson's on his way, and he's bringing a hostage negotiator with him. He said he's got one of the best in the state working out of his FBI office in Austin."

"Good."

Chance gave his mother a brief hug, nodded to Camilla, and waved them toward the turn. Carefully rounding the corner, she drove the few feet to get to the alley between rows of ranch-style houses, their backyards lined up like toy soldiers standing at attention. Each was enveloped with privacy fences, and Frank moved aside as she drove past him before stepping back into place, doing his sentry duty.

She drew in a deep breath when she reached the end of the block and pulled into the high school's parking lot. The big red fire truck was parked close to the street, at the edge of the parking lot, and several people hustled around it, setting up makeshift areas. Groups of people stood assembled in small clusters, a mix of adults and teens. It didn't look like anybody was leaving.

"Why don't you park there?" Ms. Patti motioned to a spot about a foot or so past the front end of the fire truck. "We can have a couple students carry the food to the tables. I bet they'd love to be put to work. Better than standing around worrying about your friends."

Camilla put the Escalade in park and opened the tailgate, while Ms. Patti climbed down and headed for the back. Within seconds, she'd corralled several kids, and they started unloading the food they'd prepared, handing it off in an assembly line toward the men and women manning the volunteer stations.

Her eyes scanned the crowd, searching for Heath. It

didn't take long for her to spot him. He stood several inches taller than most of the people gathered around him. Rafe stood at his side, a radio in his hand. Ridge was there, too. Though Ms. Patti hadn't mentioned it, Camilla was sure the rest of the Boudreau men were either already onsite or would arrive shortly.

They'd barely finished getting the tables set up when two pickups pulled into the parking lot and headed straight for them. Camilla recognized Douglas Boudreau behind the wheel of one, and Liam behind the wheel of the other. Douglas jumped out of his truck and sprinted toward Ms. Patti, pulling her into his arms. With the huge difference in their heights, it should have been an incongruous sight, yet the love between them was almost palpable. Douglas leaned forward and whispered something in her ear, and she shook her head.

"You doing okay, Camilla?

Liam's deep voice pulled her away from the lovely tableau she'd been watching between Douglas and Ms. Patti, and she felt a pang of remorse she didn't have somebody who'd look to her first, even in the midst of a crisis. Somebody who'd love here unconditionally, without question.

"I'm good, thanks. We haven't been here long. Your brothers are over there," she pointed toward Rafe and Heath's location. "There's been no news yet, so all I know is what your mother told me. Two men are holding a teacher and her classroom at gunpoint."

Liam nodded. "We heard the same, that's why we're here. Figured we might as well be close, in case we can help. Being on the jobsite, we'd have worried and not gotten anything done."

"I can't believe how many people are here. Wouldn't it be better if they all went home?"

Liam smiled and pushed his cowboy hat a little farther back on his head. "I doubt you'll get anybody to leave. First, this is a small town, and everybody knows everybody, and they are related to somebody who's in that classroom. Second, small town folks tend to be a little...nosy. Actually, a lot nosy, and nobody's gonna want to be left out of the loop to find out what's happening. And thirdly, when somebody in Shiloh Springs is in trouble or needs help, a good majority of the town is going to show up, ready to lend a hand."

"I guess living in a larger city, I'm not used to seeing people pulling together like this. Don't get me wrong, there are lots of wonderful and caring people where I'm from. This," she waved a hand, gesturing toward the stands of people gathered on the edge of the parking lot and spilling over onto the sidewalk, "is something I haven't seen, at least not up close and personal."

"Stick around here long enough, and you'll discover that the vast majority of people are good, decent and kindhearted. Willing to, as the saying goes, give you the shirt off their back. Now, pardon me, but I'm gonna check in with Rafe, see if there's anything I can do."

He squeezed her shoulder then sprinted away, headed toward his brothers' location. Douglas wasn't far behind him. Camilla blew out a heavy sigh, and turned back to the tables, helping Gracie get huge thermoses and disposable cups set up beside the food tables.

An idea struck, and she leaned in, whispering quickly in Gracie's ear, who nodded vigorously, and pointed to what Cam asked for. Within minutes, arms loaded, she headed across the parking lot toward Heath and Rafe. She couldn't go as fast as she wanted, because she didn't want to spill any of the coffee she carried.

Halfway there, she looked up to see Heath striding in her direction, and she broke into a smile. He lifted the cardboard box from her hands like it weighed nothing, and gave her a grin.

"Darlin', you are a lifesaver. I've been dying for a cup of coffee."

Reaching into her pocket, she pulled out a plastic bag with creamer and sweeteners. "I've got these too, since I don't know how everybody takes theirs." She pulled loose the grocery bag she'd looped around her elbow. "I've also got sandwiches, chips, and cookies. You have to eat."

"Thanks. I appreciate your thoughtfulness."

Camilla paused for a second, unsure if she should go back to the volunteer area or tag along with him and see if she could help. Her question was answered when Heath leaned forward and placed a soft kiss against her cheek.

"I've got to get back. You haul your pretty backside back over by Momma and stay safe."

"You'll call me if you need anything?"

"I promise. Now, scoot."

"Wait. Is there any news? Something I can tell your mother or the others?"

Heath's expression grew dark, and she knew whatever news he had was bleak. Even though she didn't know any of the people inside the barricaded school, her stomach tensed, anticipating his words.

"So far, we're at a standstill. We've got a professional hostage negotiator on the way, should be here in ten, maybe fifteen minutes. In the meantime, Rafe's trying to maintain calm with the two men inside with Mrs. Abernathy and her class." He shrugged, his big shoulders knotted with tension. "I hate this. We can't even get those idiots to tell us what they want or why they're doing this. Rafe and I agree, it's almost like they're waiting for something—or someone. Stalling."

Camilla blinked several times at his words. That put an entirely different spin on things, if that was the case. "If they're waiting for somebody, how do they expect that person – or persons – to get through this crowd?" She looked around at the overflowing parking lot, where a couple of deputies and volunteer fire department personnel were doing their best to keep the townspeople orderly and back from the scene.

"It'll be difficult, but we've got as many eyes on people as we can. Strangers, people who don't live in Shiloh Springs, would stand out, but strangers might think they'll blend in." Heath sounded disgruntled and unhappy. "I know it's not going to happen, but I wish people would go home until we get this resolved."

Camilla's eyes swept across the parking lot, noting most of the onlookers were gathered on the side of the school where the authorities were congregated. Very few were farther around the side of the building.

"Do you have people positioned around the other side of the school? I mean, almost everybody seems to be here," she gestured, "but what about the back, or the sides? If the two inside are really waiting for somebody, could they sneak up from a different direction, knowing y'all are occupied over here?"

"We've got a few people stationed around the sides and the back, keeping watch. I'm worried about those kids, though. The ones inside the classroom. It'll be a disaster if they decide to do something stupid." He lifted the box holding the coffee. Thanks again. I need to get back."

"Be careful, Heath. If anything happens to you…"

"Nothing's going to happen, darlin'. I promise."

He stared into her eyes, studied her face like he was trying to memorize it, and her breath caught in her throat.

Then he grinned.

"Heath?"

"Sometimes I forget how beautiful you are. And how much of a fool I've been for thinking I could live without you in my life."

Without another word, he leaned forward, pressing his lips against hers. Though the kiss was brief, it was intense, and she felt it to the tips of her toes. He turned and headed toward Rafe, and she stood frozen in place, watching him walk away.

Reeling from the emotions coursing through her, she walked toward the volunteers' area, and let her fingertips lightly skim across her lips, still feeling his kiss.

I am in so much trouble.

CHAPTER FOURTEEN

Heath handed the box filled with coffee to Jeb, taking one for himself and one for Rafe. From the slump in his brother's shoulders, it appeared they were no closer to getting things resolved than before.

"Here, you look like you need this."

"Thanks." Taking a long drink, Rafe ran his hand against the back of his neck and closed his eyes briefly. "I can't get a read on this guy. When Joel came rushing into the office, I got the impression he was talking about a couple young guys. The dude who answered the phone sounded older."

"Williamson and the negotiator should be here any minute. Maybe they'll have more success. You aren't used to dealing with these kinds of situations—they are."

Rafe spun and glared at Heath. "These are my people. Not strangers. We grew up with most of these kids' parents, went to school with them. I'm not going to sit by and let anything happen to their children. I can't."

Heath clapped his brother on the shoulder. "I know, neither can I. Listen, I want to see if I can get on the roof. I might be able to—"

"No." Rafe's voice brooked no argument.

"Yes." Heath stared at Rafe, refusing to back down. "Nobody knows how to get into this school better than I do. They haven't made a lot of structural changes since I went here. I know every nook and cranny of the upper level and the roof." He grinned before adding, "I had some of my best dates up there."

Rafe chuckled at Heath's grin. "I remember. I also remember how many times Coach Bryant kicked your behind off that roof. How much detention did you get anyway?"

"Not enough to keep me from going up there again." Heath met Rafe's stare. "I can do this. I swear I won't take any chances, but I can at least suss out the situation, give you a better read on things. Bro, it's the best chance we've got."

"Do it. You see anything, you call me ASAP. You do not enter the classroom under any circumstances. Got it?"

"Brody and Antonio are still in the back, right?" At Rafe's nod, he continued. "When I climb down from the roof, I'll try and open a couple of windows back there to give you access points."

"Get eyes on those kids, make sure they and their teacher are okay. Then we'll deal with the two intruders."

Heath gave a single nod and took off at a quick run toward the back of the high school. Whether Rafe wanted him going up to the roof or not, he knew in his gut he was the best qualified to try and get inside the locked down building. Little changes had been made, but nothing structurally, and though it had been years, he knew the layout of the school like the back of his hand.

He grinned when he spotted the rain gutter running down the side of the building. Normally he wouldn't take a chance climbing one, because he was a big guy at six foot five and two-twenty. Fortunately, the school had more than a few guys utilize the rain gutter as their own personal jungle gym, resulting in broken bones, including his own broken clavicle. They'd reinforced the entire length of the rain gutter with solid steel brackets, anchored into the wall. No way was that sucker coming down. Which meant he had a stable, ready-made ladder to the top.

"What do you think you're doing, bro?"

"Reliving my ill-spent youth," Heath answered Brody with a chuckle. "Talk to Rafe, he'll explain. I gotta go."

Without a backward glance, Heath started climbing hand-over-hand, using his feet to brace against the wall.

This was a heck of a lot easier with sneakers than boots.

Out of breath by the time he reached the top, he stood hunched over with his hands on his knees, drawing in breath. All the while his eyes scanned the rooftop, taking an inventory of what items were scattered across it. Moving a few steps forward, he looked down and saw his brothers standing where he'd been moments before, looking up. He waved, assuring them he was okay.

He walked across the roof, taking care to keep his steps light. He didn't want any sudden noise to alert the men in the classroom below. The roof access panel consisted of a square panel, metal with steel sides, reminding him of the lid on one of those cardboard banker's boxes they kept files in. He'd seen enough of those in his office back in Virginia.

Squatting down beside the opening, he slid his fingertips around the steel lip, and grinned when he felt the locking mechanism. Some things never changed, and that was a good thing. He knew once he opened it, there'd be a ladder leading down to the equipment room. All the HVAC equipment, water heaters, electric panels, and machinery that kept the school up and running were contained in that room. The heart of the school, all in one place, he mused.

Easing the access panel open took more effort that he'd expected. Guess nobody'd been up here in a while.

Or maybe I'm getting too old to pull this nonsense.

He climbed down through the opening and placed his feet on the rungs of the ladder, quickly making his way to the floor. Looking in both directions, he didn't spot anybody. In the back of his mind, he'd anticipated finding a couple of kids who'd stayed behind when the lockdown happened. It was a known fact teenagers notoriously refused to listen to authority. He knew—he'd been one of them.

He used the back stairs to the first floor, and eased open a window. Brody stood right outside. Heath doubted he'd moved a step from the time he'd climbed to the roof. A concerned frown flitted across Brody's face.

"How's it look?"

"Didn't spot any stragglers on the second floor. I'm going to make my way to the classroom, see if I can hear anything. Then I'm going into the crawlspace. I might be able to move one of the ceiling tiles, get eyes on what's going on."

"Hang on a second." Brody reached behind his back, pulled a Sig Sauer, and handed it to him. "Just in case."

"Thanks."

Before he'd taken a step, he caught movement from the corner of his eye. Brody had thrown a leg over the window jamb and begun climbing through.

"I'm coming with you." He held up his hand when Heath started to speak. "No arguments. Between the two of us, we'll have a better chance of helping."

Heath reached forward and helped Brody the rest of the way through the window. Shaking his head, he pointed at Antonio, who'd jogged forward and stood outside.

"Stay."

Antonio glowered at him. "I am not a dog. I don't respond on command."

Heath grinned and shook his finger in Antonio's face. "Sit. Stay. Good boy." Sobering quickly, he added, "You need to keep watch, until we figure out what we're dealing with."

"You get to have all the fun. I haven't gotten to pull my gun in months. All paperwork."

"Bro, let's hope that streak continues. I'm sure Serena

likes it better when you come home without bullet holes."

Antonio shook his head and rolled his eyes before giving an exaggerated sigh. "Both of you be careful."

"We will. Call Rafe and let him know we're inside."

"You got it."

Heath and Brody moved away from the window and toward the stairs. Leaning in closer to his brother, he whispered, "I want you to head to the classroom across from Mrs. Abernathy's. Stay out of sight. Let me know if anything changes."

From outside, a squeal sounded. Heath recognized it immediately as somebody turning on a bullhorn. Seconds later, a voice he didn't recognize spoke.

"This is Special Agent Salvador Guerrero of the FBI. You've got our attention. I'd like to talk with you, find out why you're inside the high school. I'm going to give you a phone number now. I'd like you to call me at that number, so we can talk." He rattled off a number, followed by silence.

After several minutes passed without any other conversation happening, Heath motioned to Brody, pointing toward the classroom he wanted the other man in, standing guard. With quick steps, he climbed the stairs. He knew there was a crawlspace between the first and second floors of the school. When he'd been a sophomore, one of the pipes had burst, flooding water into a classroom. The repairs had been made through the roof with plumbers working inside the crawlspace. All he had to do was find the way in.

After a two-minute search, he found it behind a grate in the wall. He pulled the grate off and laid it on the floor, making sure to make as little noise as possible. Inside the crawlspace, the darkness sprawled before him like a bottomless abyss. He pulled his keys from his pocket, unclipping the miniature flashlight he kept attached. Shoving the keys back into his pocket, he started forward.

It was a tight squeeze because pipes and air conditioning conduits snaked through the narrow space. He'd made it several feet then froze, the flashlight clenched between his teeth, when he heard a scratching noise ahead. The scritch, scritch sound started and stopped several times, and his heartbeat accelerated because he had a feeling he knew exactly what it meant. Son of a biscuit eater, he hated rats.

Beady little eyes caught the glare of the flashlight, reflected at him and he sighed. There was no way he could avoid the bloody things. He waved a hand toward the rat, who didn't move, almost daring him to try and get past. Gritting his teeth, he crawled forward, refusing to be cowed by a rodent no bigger than his boot.

Why'd it have to be rats?

His hand landed inches from the rat, who let out a chittering screech and scuttled away, and Heath let loose the breath he hadn't realized he'd held.

Please, no more rats. One is more than enough.

It took a few minutes to move forward enough when he heard muffled voices. He was close. Crawling another foot or so, he paused, listening intently. Mostly he heard a woman's voice, which he assumed was Mrs. Abernathy. Low pitched, she spoke softly. He didn't hear anything from the kids. He was grateful they weren't elementary school age; these high schoolers were old enough to comprehend what was happening around them. Hopefully, he didn't have any yahoos who'd try to play hero, because that was a real possibility.

He breathed a sigh when he spotted the ceiling above the classroom, happy one thing hadn't changed. The classrooms still had drop ceiling panels. Carefully, he eased up the corner of one, and slid it about two inches over, praying nobody noticed it shift. Leaning forward, he peered through the opening to the classroom below. The desks lined the walls and were pushed in front of the doors, stacked two and three high, effectively blocking them.

"Get over here."

Okay, that voice came through loud and clear. A loud gasp followed, the cry distinctly female.

Heath could make out one of the men, a gun in one hand, his other wrapped around the woman's arm. Must be Mrs. Abernathy. She was frog-marched across the classroom, though he noted she didn't struggle. Good. Nobody wanted to give them a reason to escalate the threat level.

"Get your phone out and give it to me." He shoved her toward her desk.

"Here." Pulling open a drawer, she handed it over.

Heath admired her spunk, because although she obeyed his request, she maintained a sea of calm for her students. A couple of the girls had tear-streaked faces, but the rest seemed relatively calm.

As he scanned the class, he almost gasped when his eyes met those of one of the students. A dark-haired boy, maybe fifteen, stared at him, and Heath had no trouble reading the glimmer of hope in his gaze. He raised a finger to his lips, breathing a sigh of relief when the boy nodded and looked away. Good kid.

The other hostage-taker stood by the window, peering out through an exposed corner.

"Okay, Guerrero, I'm here."

Heath couldn't hear the other side of the conversation, but could easily read the anger in the other man's face. Medium height, slender, with dirty blond hair, the man on the phone appeared to be roughly mid to late twenties. There was a hard edge, something about the way he manhandled the teacher, but Heath would've bet this wasn't his first run in with the cops.

The second man was taller, and a little bit jittery. He kept walking away from the window only to return moments later. A sallow complexion, with a face pockmarked from acne, and framed by straggly dark hair, Heath got the feeling this guy was either flying higher than a kite or in desperate need of a hit. Either way, it made him the more dangerous of the two.

He jumped when his phone vibrated in his jeans' pocket. He'd turned the ringer off before climbing to the roof. Pulling back from the opening in the roof, he slid his finger across, and read the text.

BRODY: WHAT DO YOU SEE? EVERYONE SAFE?

He didn't dare type a response, afraid it might make too much noise. Then he remembered he could swipe from letter to letter. That could work.

ME: TEACHER AND STUDENTS SCARED BUT SAFE. TWO ARMED WITH 9mm. STANDBY.

He slid the phone back in his pocket. Brody wouldn't make a move without Heath telling him to, not unless everything devolved into chaos. Better to let the hostage negotiator try to deescalate things first. Peering through the opening, he again met the eyes of the teenager who'd spotted him before. The kid jerked his head toward the front of the classroom where the teacher and the one gunman stood. The guy held the phone to his ear, scowling at whatever he heard on the other end.

"Ain't doing that, man. Anybody comes into this building, it'll be a bloodbath, I promise you."

Whatever the negotiator said on the other end must have been the right thing, because the gunman lowered his gun, and motioned for Mrs. Abernathy to go back to her students.

"You want a good faith act? Fine, I'll give you one." He pointed toward a girl with long red hair and freckles, her arm wrapped around a smaller girl with dark hair and eyes, who'd obviously been crying. "Get up."

The redhead whispered something to the other girl and stood, a defiant look on her face. "What?"

The gunman gestured with his gun, motioning to the girl she'd been comforting. "Get over here. Both of you."

The girl with dark hair gasped, and the redheaded one leaned in closer, whispering something, and the dark-haired one nodded, slowly rising to her feet. She grasped the redhead's hand and together they approached the gunman.

"You're outta here. You let the cops know we haven't hurt anybody—yet."

The redhead didn't hesitate, running for the door, practically dragging the other girl behind her. Heath grabbed his phone and quickly texted Brody, letting him know to stay put. Good thing, as it turned out, because the gunman followed them out the door, watching them.

"See that, Guerrero? I kept my word. How about you keep yours? You find Neil Perkins, get him here, or the next people coming out that door won't be in the same condition as those girls, get me? You've got thirty minutes." Without another word, he hung up.

Neil Perkins? Where do I know that name from?

He quickly texted Brody.

ME: WHO IS NEIL PERKINS?

BRODY: LIVES UP ON THE NORTHERN EDGE OF THE COUNTY WITH HIS FAMILY. WHY?

ME: GUNMAN TOLD THE NEGOTIATOR TO

FIND HIM AND GET HIM HERE.

BRODY: NO CLUE WHY. FAR AS I KNOW, GUY HASN'T BEEN IN ANY TROUBLE RECENTLY. I'LL CHECK WITH RAFE.

Camilla passed out sandwiches and chips by rote, her thoughts filled with worry. She knew Heath wanted – no, needed – to be in the middle of the crisis. That's the kind of man he was; he'd never stand by and do nothing. But this waiting, standing on the sidelines? She was about to lose her mind.

Volunteers manned the tables. Seemed like nobody had left the scene. In fact, she wouldn't be surprised if most of the town was gathered in the parking lot or lining the streets in front of the high school. Growing up in a much bigger city, she'd never experienced the kind of coming together Shiloh Springs exhibited today. The caring and giving displayed by the townspeople warmed her deep inside.

"Hon, why don't you take a break? You look like you could use one." Daisy Parker patted her shoulder. Camilla remembered her from the diner that bore her name. She'd eaten there a few times and recognized the woman with the quirky smile and the wild colors she wore in her hair. Today she had a deep purple streak through her bangs and a couple of chunky pieces on each side. Somehow the vivid color suited her personality.

"That's okay, I'd rather stay busy. Keeps me from overthinking things, you know."

"Things like Heath Boudreau?"

Camilla felt a wash of heat across her face, knew she was probably bright red. Daisy's chuckle confirmed her suspicion. Sticking her tongue out, she blew a raspberry and then laughed. "Am I that obvious?"

"Do you really want me to answer?"

"Probably not." Camilla waved a hand by her face, hoping the act would cool her burning blush. "I didn't realize everybody knows I'm...attracted to him."

Daisy bumped her hip against Camilla's. "Can't blame you, girl, he is fine. All those Boudreau men are. Lucky you, from what I've heard, he feels the same about you."

Camilla whirled to face her. "Where'd you hear that?"

"Pfft. Everybody talks in the diner. You'd be amazed at what I hear every day. There's not a day goes by one of the Boudreaus isn't in my place. They tend to forget how often I'm walking by the tables and booths. My place is a goldmine of information on everybody in this town." She fluttered her lashes, attempting to look innocent. "They're lucky I know how to keep secrets."

Camilla passed another sandwich to a person who'd walked up to her table, and pointed them to the table where drinks were being handed out.

"I can do this, Camilla. Take a break. Take a walk. You

are wound up tighter than a jack-in-the-box about to pop. If you're lucky, you might run into a tall, handsome man while you're at it."

Camilla took a deep breath and stepped away from the table, letting Daisy take her spot. Maybe she was right. She felt like she was about to combust. She'd always thought writing tense situations where the hero or heroine were in peril seemed cliché, because they always solved the problem with little to no bloodshed and fell into one another's arms. This—real life—was nothing like her books. Nothing she'd written came close to the angst and heartache she saw scrawled on the faces of the parents with children locked in the classroom with armed gunmen. The palpable stress of their fellow classmates who'd made it out of the school was thick in the air. There was no joviality in the air, no laughter or boisterous joking amongst the teens.

Without conscious thought, she found herself closer to where she'd last spotted Heath, though he was nowhere to be seen. Rafe stood huddled with two other men, neither of which she recognized. From his serious expression, things weren't looking good.

One of the strangers straightened, a bullhorn in his hand. He must be the FBI hostage negotiator.

"This is Special Agent Salvador Guerrero of the FBI. You've got our attention. I'd like to talk with you, find out why you're inside the high school. I'm going to give you a phone number now. I'd like you to call me at that number, so we can talk." He gave a phone number and lowered the bullhorn.

Where's Heath? I can't believe he's not here in the middle of things. I hope he's not doing something stupid.

She wrapped her arms across her middle, feeling a sudden chill race down her spine. The idea Heath might be doing something crazy and heroic and decidedly dangerous crept into her thoughts. Would he? She barely refrained from rolling her eyes. What was she thinking? Of course he'd stride right into the middle of a hostage crisis. Hadn't he flung himself into the middle of her insanity with a shooter?

"Please, please be careful, you idiot."

Now all she could do was wait and pray he didn't do something stupid.

CHAPTER FIFTEEN

Heath kept his eyes glued to the scene below him, feeling the tension ratchet up. Several minutes had passed since the first hostages had been released, and he hadn't heard back from Brody yet. Which meant Heath had no clue who Neil Perkins was, and why the two men figured holding a classroom filled with teenagers seemed like a good idea.

When the phone in his hand vibrated, he jerked, hitting his head against the HVAC ductwork. Crudité on a cracker, that hurt! Looking at the caller ID, he winced when he saw Shiloh's name. His brother was probably calling about the situation with Renee, but no matter how much he'd like to get an update on his search, it'd have to wait.

Slowly crawling forward, he shifted the ceiling tile another inch. One gunman, the one who'd followed the hostages down the hall, now leaned against the teacher's desk, the 9mm clasped loosely in his hand. The other man wasn't visible, which really bugged him.

"Perkins isn't gonna get away with double-crossing us. Does he think we're stupid? Like I'm going to walk away from all that money, let him keep everything. We did all the work. We took all the risks. I'm not going back to the boss and tell him we screwed up. Nuh-uh. I like my head attached to my body."

The other man, still out of Heath's range of sight answered. "Little cockroach ain't gonna be able to hide. We'll get our stuff, and then squash him like the dirty bug he is. Nobody's getting away with playing fast and loose with what's ours."

Heath listened intently, trying to make heads or tails of what the two bad guys said. Seemed like they were tap-dancing around, no mention of what Neil Perkins had of theirs or why he'd double-crossed them. Color him surprised, there was no honor among thieves.

A short vibration of his phone alerted him to a text message.

BRODY: NEIL PERKINS' FATHER IS OUTSIDE TALKING TO RAFE. NOBODY'S SEEN NEIL. WHAT'S GOING ON?

ME: TENSE. GUYS TALKING ABOUT NEIL HAVING SOMETHING BELONGS TO THEM. THEY WANT IT BACK.

BRODY: WHY TAKE HOSTAGES THOUGH?

That was something Heath had been wondering, too. A sudden thought had him texting his question to Brody.

ME: HOW OLD IS NEIL PERKINS? COULD HE BELONG IN THIS CLASS?

BRODY: WHOA! LET ME CHECK.

Looking down through the small opening in the ceiling tile, he still couldn't see the second gunman. He blinked when he saw the kid from earlier, leaning back in his chair like he didn't have a care in the world, watching him through the hole. When he noticed Heath's scowl, he grinned and winked. Heath ignored him and looked at Brody's text.

BRODY: NEIL ISN'T IN MS. ABERNATHY'S CLASS. BUT HIS BROTHER IS. GUESS NEIL HELPED HIM DITCH TODAY. OR KNEW HIS BUDDIES WERE LOOKING FOR HIM, AND THOUGHT THEY MIGHT GO AFTER HIS BRO.

Before Heath could answer, a phone rang inside the classroom, answered almost instantly.

"You better have good news, Guerrero. Where's Perkins?"

An ugly scowl appeared on the man's face, followed by a string of some of the foulest curse words he'd ever heard spewed from him. The other gunman moved to stand at his side, his face reddened with anger. Uh oh, this wasn't good.

"What's up?"

"Stupid feds can't find Neil. So help me, if he's run off with my stuff, I'm gonna hunt him down and blow his brains out."

"How are we gonna get out of here if we don't have Perkins? His brother was our leverage, and he ain't here."

"I don't know, I gotta think."

The first gunman held the cell phone against his forehead, and Heath could almost hear the wheels turning in his head. Sure sounded like Perkins held their stash of drugs, but Heath's gut didn't think it was that easy. Didn't make sense to hold a classroom hostage for a drug deal gone bad. No, this was bigger.

The phone in the classroom rang again, immediately was answered by the gunman.

"What?" An ugly laugh emerged from his mouth, directed at whoever was on the other end of the line. "Perkins, you lousy S.O.B., where are you? Buck and I showed up. Waited for you. When you didn't show, figured you'd run off."

Heath grabbed his phone and texted Brody, letting him know Perkins was on Mrs. Abernathy's phone, talking to the gunman and to let Rafe know. He watched both men closely. The first man paced in front of the desk, irritation painting an ugly expression on his already ugly mug.

"No more games, Perkins. You've got fifteen minutes to get to the high school, or…well, you don't want to know or what, bud. Fifteen. Minutes."

Whatever Perkins said on the other end didn't make dude number one happy, because his face turned red, and he sputtered out another string of curses. He raised the phone, his intent clear, but number two grabbed his arm, wrenching the phone from his hand.

"Man, are you crazy? You destroy the phone, how're we

gonna know when Perkins gets here? Chill, dude."

Heath pulled out his phone and texted Brody.

ME: GUNMAN TOLD NEIL TO BE HERE IN FIF-
TEEN MINUTES. LET RAFE KNOW.

BRODY: GOT IT.

ME: BE READY, BRO. I THINK THINGS ARE
ABOUT TO HIT THE FAN.

BRODY: I'VE GOT YOUR BACK.

"Hey, I got to use the restroom." The kid who'd spotted
Heath earlier yelled to the gunman. "Can't hold it anymore."

"Tough, kid. Nobody's going anywhere."

"Dude, I've held it as long as I can." The kid stood and
walked up, getting right in the other man's face. "Look, I'm
not going to pee my pants in front of the girls. Either one of
you takes me to the head or shoot me."

"What is this, a bloody kindergarten?" The gunman
looked at his partner and jerked his head toward the door.
"Take the crybaby to the head."

Heath hoped the kid didn't try to pull anything. Unfortunately, from the way the kid had been watching him, he
wasn't holding out hope he didn't think he could play hero.

ME: ONE OF THE GUNMEN IS TAKING A KID
TO THE BATHROOM. KEEP YOUR EYES OPEN.

BRODY: GOT IT.

He wished he could follow and take out the guy, but he
needed eyes on the one still in the classroom. He seemed to
be the leader. When the phone inside the classroom rang

again, he almost jumped. Couldn't be Perkins again minutes hadn't passed.

"What?" The gunman listened intently, not saying a word. One hand held the phone, while the other—the one holding the gun—rubbed along the side of his face. "Guerrero, you heard from Perkins yet? Time's almost up. I'd hate to have to start sending kids out in body bags."

Shocked gasps echoed through the classroom, and a couple of the girls started crying. The guy was getting fidgety and Heath knew he needed to make a move soon, before things erupted in chaos.

BRODY: WHO IS THIS KID? HE PULLED SOME KUNG-FU JUJITSU MOVE IN THE BATHROOM. TOOK OUT THE GUNMAN WITH A SINGLE KICK TO THE HEAD. THIS BAD GUY OUT OF THE PICTURE. I'M TAKING THE KID AND THIS JERK OUT THE BACK TO ANTONIO. YOU SEE AN OPENING, MAKE YOUR MOVE, BRO.

ME: THANKS. TELL RAFE TO STAND BY. IF I GET A CHANCE, I'M TAKING THIS ONE OUT.

The gunman started pacing back and forth in front of the desk, and Mrs. Abernathy walked toward the front slowly, approaching him like she was approaching a rabid animal, her hands held open at her sides. Please, don't do anything stupid, Heath thought. With one man down, he was running out of time to make a move before this guy noticed.

"Sir? Please, you're scaring the kids."

"Lady, sit down and shut up, or you'll be the first one going out feet first, got it?"

"These children are my responsibility. They're terrified enough without you waving that gun around. I don't think you want to shoot one of them accidentally. We're all wanting a good resolution, and everybody getting out of her safe. Scaring helpless children won't look good to the authorities."

"Lady, I ain't worried about what local cops think. All I want is my guns, and nobody is getting out of here until I have them."

Guns? I knew this was about more than drugs.

"Where's Dwight?"

"Is that the other man? He hasn't come back from the restroom yet." Mrs. Abernathy glanced toward the door, and Heath could practically read her mind, worrying about where the kid had disappeared to.

"Son of a…" He loped to the door, sticking his head out to look down the hall, yelling, "What's taking so long, Dwight?"

When no answer came back, the gunman's complexion turned ruddy, and he spun around, his eyes wild. Heath knew time had run out. He couldn't wait any longer. When Mrs. Abernathy took a step back from the gunman, Heath shoved the ceiling panel aside, and launched himself through the opening, landing atop the man, and slamming his knees against the floor. Hard.

Straddling the gunman, he grabbed at the hand holding the gun, struggling for the gun. He could hear Mrs. Abernathy's voice, ushering the kids out the classroom, saw dozens of pairs of feet racing past, but he couldn't afford to let up. The man beneath him bucked, trying to throw Heath off. Wouldn't work. Heath had ridden more than one ornery bronco when he was younger, and never got thrown. This two-legged varmint didn't have a chance.

Wrapping his hand around the other's wrist, he banged his hand against the floor, once, twice, and wrenched the gun from his hand. Still he struggled, refusing to relent. Heath tossed the gun aside, far out of reach, and slammed his fist against the gunman's face, and watched his eyes roll back in his head.

Once he knew the guy was out cold, he grabbed his phone, and dialed Rafe.

"Heath, what's happening?"

"All clear in here. Brody got one and I've taken out the other."

Within seconds, the halls were awash with bodies. Rafe and Antonio skidded to a stop right inside the doorway, and noted Heath still sitting atop the bad guy. Rafe's laugh diffused the last of the tension, and he walked over to Heath, who stood up, allowing Rafe to slap the cuffs on the guy.

"Good job, bro."

"Thanks, but I had help. Brody deserves a lot of credit.

He and one of the kids took out the first gunman, so I was able to get the drop on this one."

"I heard. Brody's fine, not a scratch on him. The kid's name is Gilbert. A bit of a hothead, but basically a good guy. His parents are out there, hailing him as a hero, and he's eating it up."

Heath leaned against the desk, feeling the ache starting in his knees. He'd landed hard, and he'd be bruised, but it was worth it.

"Neil Perkins show up yet?" At Rafe's questioning look, he continued. "The gunmen talked to him. Said he has their guns."

"Guns? This was about guns?"

Heath nodded. "Apparently Perkins has their guns. When the deal went south, they came here looking for Perkins' little brother, who's in Mrs. Abernathy's class." He straightened. "Since there are guns involved, I'm gonna need to talk to Perkins, and call this into the Austin ATF. Figure out where the guns came from, how many we're talking about." He chuckled and slapped Rafe on the shoulder. "Here I thought I was on vacation, and I'm going to have to work. Awesome."

Heath stepped aside as the investigative team piled through the door and noted there were the local guys as well as strangers in FBI windbreakers. Glad he didn't have to deal with the fallout of this mess, and he didn't envy his brother. Once he notified the ATF, he'd get to go home with

Camilla.

Funny how his heart skipped a beat when he thought about Cam. Knowing she was outside, waiting and worrying for him, had him walking faster. He needed to see her face, hold her in his arms, and set his world right.

Walking outside, he shielded his eyes with his hand, instinctively searching for Camilla. He limped toward the sheriff's car, his eyes scanning the crowded parking lot looking for her. The breath caught in his chest when he saw her standing beside his mother. Safe. She was safe.

Rafe moved to stand beside him. "She's fine. Helpful gal; she passed out food, made sure the people working the scene were taken care of. You picked a good one."

Heath couldn't agree more. But for now, work came first. "I need to talk to Neil Perkins. Where is he?"

"I had Dusty take him to the station. We're gonna get to the bottom of this and find out what he's doing in the middle of a hostage situation."

"ATF will handle the guns. I'll call and get somebody here ASAP."

"Works for me. I want to know what's happening, so keep me posted. If Perkins and his buddies think they're going to run guns through my county, they'll be quickly disabused from that belief."

"Give me a couple of minutes to talk to Momma and Cam, and then we can head for the station, and get this over with."

"Go."

Even though he hurt from landing on the gunman, Heath jogged over to wrap his arms around his mother first, hugging her close. After a couple minutes of assuring her everything was okay, he turned to Camilla.

Without hesitating, she flung herself into his arms, her body trembling. He pulled her close, feeling his world right itself on its axis. With Cam in his arms, he knew everything would be alright.

He was home.

CHAPTER SIXTEEN

Camilla stood on the front porch of the Big House, leaning against one of the pillars, and studied the vast green expanse stretching as far as she could see. How big the property was she couldn't imagine, nor did she care. She simply took in the unvarnished beauty surrounding her. Being here, surrounded by nature's miraculous display, a sense of peace invaded her, filling her with the familiar warmth she'd come to associate with the Boudreaus.

She'd been trying to write, but the words simply wouldn't come. That rarely happened, and it wasn't a feeling she was used to. What little she'd been able to put on the computer screen had been garbage, and she refused to give her readers anything less than the best she could do. Needing to clear her mind, and maybe come up with a new way to look at the scene she needed to write, she'd decided to get some fresh air and appreciate the tranquility.

She took a sip of the sweet tea she'd brought out, a little smile tugging at her lips. Sweet tea was a southern thing, and she'd become addicted to the beverage, since Ms. Patti seemed to always have a pitcher sitting in the fridge.

"What are you up to, pretty girl?"

The deep rumble of Heath's voice slid over her like a silken caress, and she shivered. That sexy southern drawl did something to her insides. Turning slowly, she gave him a welcoming smile. The day before at the high school had been horrid, and she couldn't imagine how tough it had been on Heath. He hadn't gotten back to the Big House until the wee hours of the morning. Not that she was going to admit lying awake, waiting to hear him come in the front door.

"Taking a break. The scene's not working for me, and I'm dissecting it, trying to figure out where I took a wrong turn."

"I've no doubt you'll work it out, and it'll be great."

"Thanks." She took another sip of tea, not because she was thirsty, but simply for something to do. There was a nervous, jittery feeling in the pit of her stomach, like a thousand butterflies flittered around, tickling her from the inside. "I've got deadlines, but my brain couldn't concentrate. I figured coming out here and taking in the serenity might help."

"I love it here." He waved his arm, indicating the front of the plantation house and the land beyond. The huge live oaks spread out on each side, and she heard the pride in his voice. "Sometimes I pinch myself to make sure I'm not dreaming. I've had good and bad things happen in my life. Everybody does. But I was one of the lucky ones. I got adopted by two of the most amazing people in the world."

Beth had talked with Camilla when she'd first been introduced to the Boudreaus, during the brouhaha Evan caused her and Tessa. She'd take much of what Beth said about the Boudreaus with a grain of salt. Nobody could be as *perfect* as Beth declared. Once she met them, she was slowly concluding they were even better than Beth claimed.

"I think all of you ended up with awesome parents."

The writer part of her brain couldn't help wondering about Heath's story. She'd heard the ones for a few of the brothers. Tessa had told her about Rafe's story, with his permission of course, and Beth talked to her about Brody, knew they'd adored the Boudreau family as much as Heath. It must be nice to have that kind of sibling camaraderie. She'd only had Evan, and nobody could claim he'd been the ideal brother. A wave of guilt swept through her. Why hadn't she seen what he'd been capable of? He'd nearly killed her two best friends, and she'd never admitted she'd seen his uglier side long ago. If anything had happened, she'd never have forgiven herself.

"Earth to Cam." Heath's fingertips swept along her cheek, his touch gentle as a butterfly wing.

"Oops, sorry. I sometimes get lost in my own world, and everything fades away."

Heath held out his hand, palm up. "Take a walk with me?"

"I'd love to." Kneeling, she placed her glass by the column, straightened, and took his hand. The strength and warmth in his grasp felt oddly soothing. No matter what, she always felt safe when she was around Heath.

Climbing down the porch steps, Heath directed her to the left, the opposite direction of what she'd expected. She'd assumed he'd want to head toward the barn and the pasture, which would have been in the opposite direction. With an internal shrug, she allowed him to lead. After all, he knew the ranch like the back of his hand, and being with him was more than enough.

Looking down at their clasped hands, Heath winked at her and she grinned. With a gentle tug, they rounded the corner of the house, and she saw the lovely porch with a table and chairs. Colorful flowers bloomed and cascaded around the sides of ceramic and glass pots. Somebody had a green thumb.

They continued walking toward a huge stand of pine trees and began making their way deeper into the wooded area. Heath stepped in front of her and turned. She stopped.

"Do you trust me?" His voice was a low hush, almost a whisper. At her nod, he continued. "Close your eyes."

"What?"

"It's a surprise. I promise you'll like it. Come on, pretty girl, close your eyes."

"Alright, Goober. I'll play along."

As her eyes closed, he took both of her hands in his and drew her forward. She did trust him. Knew he wouldn't let her fall or trip on the forest's overgrown roots or nearly invisible rocks.

Less than a minute later, he stopped. When she started to open her eyes, he moved closer. "Don't open them yet." Releasing her hands, she felt more than heard him move around behind her. Within seconds, his hands rested atop her shoulders.

"Okay, you can open your eyes."

The breath caught in the back of her throat as she beheld the prettiest gazebo she'd ever seen. Surrounded by tall pine trees and smaller bushes, the scene was like something out of a fairytale. The only thing missing was a castle in the background and a knight in shining armor. Drawing in a deep breath, the fragrance of roses swept across her senses. The heady floral scent should have seemed out of place in this forested glade. Instead, it blended into the magic of the scene.

"It's beautiful."

"This is Momma's secret garden. She's worked on it, pampered it, for as long as I've lived here."

Taking a step forward, Camilla ran her fingertips along the coolness of the white-painted wood. The roses trailed up toward the gazebo's ceiling, climbing along the columns, giving the whole scene an enchanted feel, like she'd entered a fairytale garden. It certainly didn't resemble anything like she'd expect to find in Central Texas, but somehow it fit perfectly.

"Your mother did this? It's breathtaking. I'd love to have

a special place like this to relax after a long day of writing, but I'm afraid I don't have a green thumb. It's not that I kill every plant I touch. I simply get caught up in the story I'm working on and kind of forget to water them until it's too late."

Heath chuckled softly. "I'm guilty of that, too. I've stopped trying to raise anything in my apartment. I have a little window box, and I kept refilling it every spring, and by summertime I'd have to toss them."

She walked around the gazebo, taking in all the plants and ornamental grasses planted with loving care. The white-painted lattice that skirted the bottom provided a backdrop for the colorful flora.

"Watch this." Heath flipped a switch inside the opening to the gazebo, and tiny fairy lights flickered on. Though it wasn't dark, she could imagine what it would look like. Dusk would be a perfect time to come out here and sit inside, the petite white lights glistening like stars.

Heath held out his hand, and she slid hers into his, feeling the warmth as his engulfed hers. Leading her up the few steps, he guided her into the gazebo. For the first time, she noticed at the center of the building sat a wishing well. Unlike the rest of the gazebo, which was painted a crisp, bright white, the wishing well's wooden supports had been left to weather with age. Instead of being a deep brown, the wood had a variegated cavalcade of colors from brown to muted gray.

Looking down into the depths of the well, she couldn't help wishing she had a coin to toss into its watery depths. She'd bet making a wish here would come true. Glancing at the tall man standing beside her, she knew exactly what she'd wish for.

As if reading her mind, he reached into his pocket and pulled out a quarter, grinning when she snatched it out of his hand.

"What are you going to wish for?"

She shook her finger in front of his face. "No way I'm telling you. Don't you know if you tell your wish, it won't come true?" Closing her eyes, she concentrated for a few seconds, thinking about wording her wish to make sure it was perfect. With a flick of her wrist, she tossed the quarter into the well.

"Think it'll come true?" Heath's sapphire eyes held a hint of laughter, and she couldn't hold back a smile.

"I hope so."

Heath walked to the side of the gazebo and lowered himself onto one of the built-in benches encircling the inside. He patted the seat next to him. When she joined him, he took her hand again and she couldn't help wondering why he'd been so touchy-feely recently.

"I'd like to tell you a story."

The seriousness in his tone made her answer a bit more cautiously than she might have, considering their earlier flirtation. She couldn't imagine what he might want to share, but from his expression and his tone, it was important. "Okay."

"There's one thing I've got to know before I do."

"What's that?"

"What it feels like to kiss you. May I kiss you, pretty girl?"

He wanted to *kiss* her? Asking permission? Slowly, her tongue slid along her lips in an unconscious movement, and she nodded.

His slow smile was the last thing she saw as her lids lowered, and he brushed his lips against hers. At first, the touch felt light, almost like a whisper against her skin. After a moment, he deepened the kiss, and she melted in his arms, her lips parting. Everything within her responded to his touch, though he didn't demand more than she was willing to give.

When he pulled back, her fingers brushed against her lips, and she watched the tiniest smile tug at the corner of his mouth. Darn him, he knew exactly what his kiss had done to her. From the slightly glazed look in his eyes, she guessed he felt the same. At least, she hoped so.

Taking a deep breath, she cupped her hands around his face and pulled him down for another soul-stealing kiss, holding back nothing. She poured everything she felt into that kiss, refusing to let her fears obliterate the passion coursing through her. Feeling him respond made her pulse race, and she wanted to keep this feeling forever. Preserve it, like a moment out of time.

Finally breaking the kiss, she drew in a shaky breath, her whole body trembling. Wow, she'd never expected to feel the rush of excitement, the desire coursing through her at something as simple as a first kiss. Thinking about it, she realized there was nothing simple about her feelings for Heath.

"That was…intense."

Heath nodded. "I had the feeling if we ever gave in, we'd be combustible. Guess I was right." He brushed a lock of hair behind her ear, and she shivered when his skin touched her.

"I'm not sure—"

He placed a finger against her lips. "I have a story to tell you. After, if you still want to talk, we'll talk."

"Alright."

In a move that surprised her, he pulled her to his side, wrapped his arm around her, with her head resting against his shoulder. Snuggling in, she waited for him to begin his tale.

Heath's heartbeat raced in his chest, still feeling the echo of Camilla's lips touching his. The lingering taste of her kiss had him wishing he could dive back in and worship her lips. His feelings for the beautiful woman had only grown and intensified the more he'd gotten to know her. Though they hadn't spent any long periods of time together, when they were in the same room together, it was like insta-lust, because he wanted to claim her, make her his in every conceivable way. Heck, he'd get her name tattooed over his heart to proclaim how he felt—and he was terrified of needles.

"How much do you know about my family? How we all ended up together living with the Boudreaus?"

"I know what Beth and Tessa have told me, so it's mostly been about Rafe and Brody. You mother has told me a bit too, but not many details. I...didn't want to pry."

"In other words, your curiosity is killing you to dig, but you haven't?"

Camilla chuckled. "Pretty much. You've gotta admit, the whole thing with your family taking in troubled young boys, most of them from pretty rough backgrounds, is the stuff great stories are made of."

He shrugged and snuggled her a little closer. "I guess. If you'd like to hear it, I want to share mine with you."

When she lifted her face toward him and met his eyes, he saw something in hers that told him everything would be okay. She'd listen and wouldn't judge him. Somehow deep in his gut, Heath knew she'd understand. Maybe she wouldn't agree with all his choices, but he hadn't been the easiest child to raise.

"My life started out probably not what you'd expect. I

was born prematurely to a crack-addicted mother. Nobody had a clue who my father might be, since my biological mother—well, let's say she had quite a number of possible candidates. She'd turn tricks, lie, steal, whatever it took to get her next fix. I became one of the thousands of kids tossed into the system by a parent who couldn't care less what happened to me."

"Heath, I'm so sorry. I had no idea."

"Most people outside the Boudreaus don't, unless they were one of the many foster homes I matriculated through. I remember every single one of them, could tell you precisely how long my stay in their care lasted, down to the day. Some of them tried, I'll give them an A for effort, but I wasn't the easiest child. I had a lot of issues growing up. Battling an addiction along with a couple of other health issues at birth and during my first two years of life made things rough."

When Camilla reached for his hand and squeezed it, he nearly groaned. He hated telling people about how he'd grown up. Most of his early years, his formative years, were spent in rebellion. Rage at his mother, who hadn't wanted him. Rage at an institutional system that was overcrowded, underfunded, and understaffed to be able to do much except babysit. Rage at himself because no matter how hard he tried, he could never be the perfect little boy people wanted and expected.

"I won't sugarcoat things because you deserve the truth. The whole unvarnished good, bad, and ugly things that make up who I am. Like I said, the first few years of my life were spent keeping me alive and getting healthy. Once I started mixing in with the rest of the kids, it never got any easier. I'd been a premature birth, but when I hit four, I started growing. By the time I was five, I was far bigger than anybody else my age. And I was a mean little cuss. A bully. Rotten to the core. Violent. Lots of anger issues."

"It's hard to picture that. I know with your size," she patted a hand on his biceps, "people might interpret you as hard, but you've never been anything but kind and gentle with me."

"I doubt you thought that when we first met," Heath chuckled, remembering their fiery back and forth on Camilla's first visit to Shiloh Springs. It certainly had its defining moments.

"I was never afraid of you. Pissed at you, sure, because you did everything you could to get under my skin. You took my laptop. Teased me mercilessly. Flirted with everybody else, but not me." Her gaze met his directly. "Honestly, I wondered if I'd done something to piss you off, because you would flirt outrageously with Tessa, Beth, and Serena, but never me."

He squeezed her hand, the one she still clasped. "It wasn't anything you'd done, I swear. I tend to flirt; it's almost an unconscious thing now, because it keeps others at a safe distance. I know they don't take it seriously. With you, I couldn't do that. Even from the very start, I knew you were different. I didn't want to be superficial with you. The flirting keeps an invisible wall up I don't cross. With you, Cam, I refused to build that divider. Deep down, I always felt we'd be more than friends. Even when I fought it tooth and nail, the feeling never went away."

"That makes a kind of sense, I guess. You weren't the only one. I felt off-kilter from the beginning because I was attracted to you. I fought it because I had my life planned out, knew where I wanted to be in five years, ten years, and a romantic entanglement wasn't part of my goals. I knew you were going to be trouble, and figured walking away was better than giving in."

"Walking away? Sweetheart, you lit out of here like your tail was on fire. I turned around and you were gone. I had to hear from Beth that you'd hightailed it home."

"I felt bad about leaving like that."

Heath put a fingertip beneath her chin and tilted it up until she met his gaze. "You ran away. It took everything I had not to hop on my bike and chase you all the way back to North Carolina."

"That probably wouldn't have been the best idea."

He sighed. "I know. Just letting you know things might have been different if I'd followed my gut."

"Finish telling me about your life before the Boudreaus." She shifted on the bench until she was smashed against his side, never turning his hand loose.

"Where was I? Oh, yeah. I'd been assigned to another

social worker. Went through them like used Kleenex. I'd be placed in a foster home, and it didn't take long for me to act out. I never lasted anyplace long, because I was a horrible mess. I went through eight different homes in the same number of years." He wrapped a lock of her hair around his finger, marveling at the silky softness. It reminded him of the satin sheets his momma used in the spare bedroom for guests. "I was a monster. No, don't shake your head. I've had years to look back at my bad attitude, always having a chip on my shoulder."

"I wish I'd know you then."

His harsh laugh sounded curt, even to his own ears. "No, you don't. I hated everyone and everything. Refused to let anybody close. Like I said, chip on my shoulder and an attitude geared toward me landing in prison before I turned eighteen. Then I met Douglas and Patricia Boudreau."

"How'd that happen?"

"The grace of God. That's what I tell myself. I didn't even live in Shiloh Springs. I was born in Dallas and had no connection to anybody here. My case file caught the attention of one of the social workers, who took one look at it and knew I'd never make it without some unconventional help."

Thinking about Alice Farmer made him smile. Barely taller than Ms. Patti, she was an African American dynamo who got things done. Her methods weren't always by the books, but she'd helped put more children with the right foster parents than anybody he knew. She'd finally retired a couple of years prior, but that didn't mean she didn't keep her finger on the pulse of all "her kids". They still exchanged Christmas cards every year.

"Well, whoever helped you deserves my thanks. I've personally never dealt with the foster care system, but in the press all you hear are the horror stories. I know there are lots of foster families out there that are wonderful, caring people, but I never met any until I met yours."

"Alice Farmer, or Mrs. A as I called her, had a brother who was in the military. His handle was Gizmo, and he was a wizard with anything electronic. Still is, according to Dad. Gizmo and my dad go way back, to their military days. Anyway, Mrs. A talked to her brother about my case, and how she saw something—she called it a spark—basically using him as a sounding board. Gizmo listened to her, and said he knew exactly where I belonged. Gave her Dad's name and number. When she called him, explained my case, he drove to Dallas that same afternoon to meet with me. Pretty much before I could blink, I was in Shiloh Springs, plunked down in the middle of an honest to goodness Texas ranch."

He paused for a breath, inhaling the scent of her shampoo. It had a citrusy scent, and he felt a wave of contentment flood him. Wound tight at the beginning of his story, he felt his coiled muscle unclench, and a sense of peace filled him. Cam knew the truth about him. He wasn't anybody's Prince Charming, riding up on a white steed ready to rescue the princess. If anything, he was gutter trash who'd managed to pull himself out of the muck with the help of parents who had loved and believed in him from the beginning.

"That must have been traumatizing, to be plucked out of an untenable situation and dropped into a totally new environment hundreds of miles away from everything you knew." Her small hand still rested in his, and she squeezed it gently. An unexpected warmth flooded him at the simple touch.

"You might say that. I didn't exactly fit in with the others. I made their lives a walking, talking, living nightmare. I was rebellion on two legs, and wasn't having any of the happy-happy baloney. It was fake, and they were only in it for the money the foster care system paid them. None of it mattered. If I acted out the way I'd done at every previous foster family, they'd soon send me back, and I'd be no better off than I'd been. I actually expected it to happen fast, because they had other kids who needed attention."

"Guess it didn't work out the way you'd planned."

Heath could hear the smile in Camilla's voice. Her reaction to him spilling all his secrets surprised him. Then again, he wasn't really sure what he'd expected. But he'd yet to see the one thing he'd dreaded. Pity.

"It's funny. The more I rebelled, the more love I got from the Boudreaus. Momma would hug me every time I walked in the door. Course she'd also give me what for when I acted out. I was a walking, talking advertisement for a juvenile delinquent. I got into fights with Rafe and Antonio constantly. The first month I lived here, I don't think there was a day that went by one of us wasn't sporting a black eye or a bloody nose. Brody usually played the peacemaker, but he's always been the boy scout."

"He's good with Beth and Jamie. I know she's crazy about him."

Heath made a scoffing noise. "My brother adores the ground Beth walks on. Watching those two lovebirds is enough to give me cavities."

He felt her body shaking against his, knew she was biting back her laughter. He almost wished she let it free; it was a beautiful sound.

Camilla nudged him gently with her elbow. "Go on, Goober."

"No matter how hard I tried, I couldn't get Momma and Dad to send me away. I gave it everything I had, tantrum, running away. You name it, I tried it. Finally, after I'd been here a little over a month, I finally broke. I cornered Momma in the kitchen. Dad was sitting at the table; he'd stopped home for lunch. I stormed in, a fire in my belly. I couldn't take it anymore, waiting for them to send me back to Dallas. Back to where I belonged." He cringed at the memories flooding through him, multicolored and vivid, a kaleidoscope of pictures racing through his brain. "Momma stood at the sink, her arms up to her elbows in soapy water. She hummed some old song softly. Dad watched her every move, so much love in his gaze it made me physically cringe. All I knew was I had to get away from them, because I felt deep in my gut if I hung around, my life would change. It was as inevitable as the tide coming in or the sun rising and setting. From my perspective, change was bad. Change meant being shuffled off someplace, never settling, never feeling. Always angry because I wasn't wanted."

"But they wanted you."

"Try telling that to my immature brain. I could see all the love they showed to their other sons. They were wanted. They were loved. They would never again know what it's like to feel alone. I skidded to a halt inside the hall, looking into the kitchen, and something inside me exploded. It felt like I was consumed by flames, burning to ashes where I stood. There was this volcanic rush, and I screamed at the top of my lungs. Scared Momma bad enough she dropped the plate she was washing. Shattered into pieces. Dad jumped from the table, raced straight at me. I braced, expecting to feel his fist."

He felt her vehement head shake against his shoulder, though she didn't say a word. Hiding his smile, he pressed a brief kiss against the top of her head.

"You're right. Expecting to feel pain, because Dad's a big guy, instead he shocked me to the core. He wrapped his arms around me, pulling me in tight and demanding to know what had happened. I struggled against him, but he refused to turn me loose. I screamed and fought like a wildcat, punching and clawing, but he never let go. Heck, I have no idea what I'd have done if I'd managed to get free." Heath chuckled. "You've seen my dad. In my addled juvenile brain, I thought I could take him. The man's a walking mountain."

"You're not a slouch yourself," she murmured softly.

"I don't know how long we stood there, with me fighting him like my life depended on it. Maybe it did. I heard Momma crying softly, and it finally got through my thick head she was crying for me. *For me.* That was my epiphany moment. I stopped fighting, and Dad slowly turned loose. I remember asking when they'd send me back to Dallas. The expression on my mother's face? I don't think I could have hurt her more if I'd struck her. Dad simply stood there slowly shaking his head. 'Son,' he said, 'what makes you think we'd ever send you away? You're ours.' It finally sank in: no matter how hard I pushed, how awful I acted, they weren't going to throw me away like everybody else. I'd finally come home."

Shock filled him when Camilla turned in his arms and buried her face against his shoulder, and he could hear her quietly sobbing. His arms tightened around her.

"Hey, I didn't mean to make you cry."

"Have I told you how much I love your parents?"

"I do, too."

They sat quietly for a time, simply being with each other. Telling Camilla about his rotten childhood had been cathartic in a way he hadn't anticipated, and he felt a weight lift off his heart. She hadn't judged him and left him feeling unwanted. Guess it was leftover guilt or maybe fear of abandonment that never quite went away, but he'd secretly been terrified if she knew the whole truth, she'd walk away.

But what about when things were settled, and she could go home again? Closing his eyes, he pondered the bigger question—did they—could they have chance at a future together?

CHAPTER SEVENTEEN

"You sure?"

"Heath, I'm not some rookie who doesn't know his head from his backside." Jeb's voice held more than a touch of defensiveness. "You asked me to keep my eyes open, and let you know if I spotted anybody around town who looked suspicious."

"Sorry. This whole situation has got me on edge. Tell me what you saw."

Heath picked up his cup, drank the rest of the coffee, and waved at Daisy for a refill. He'd driven into town early. He had a lot on his plate to handle today, and meeting up with Jeb hadn't been on his list of things to do. Jeb waved him down as he'd headed into the sheriff's station, and they'd walked to the diner together.

"Doing my rounds, I noticed a couple of cars in the B&B's parking lot. Nothing odd about that, I know. One is a rental out of Houston, and before you ask, yes, I checked the plate, which is how I know it's from Houston. I've got the info on that, but I doubt you'll need it. The other car has Louisiana plates."

Heath's body went on alert at the mention of Louisiana. Could be a coincidence. After all, they were the next state over, and people from there drove into Texas all the time. But his instincts, his intuition, that special knack which kept him on the balls of his feet when something big was about to happen, pinged inside his skull.

"Tell me about the Louisiana car. Did you run those plates?"

"Yep. Vehicle went missing two days ago in New Orleans. Owners reported it stolen last night. They thought their teenage son took it out joyriding with his buddies. When he came home and they discovered he didn't have their car, they reported it to the police."

"Is it still in the B&B parking lot?"

Jeb nodded. "It was twenty minutes ago."

Daisy stood beside their table with a coffee pot in her hand and began refilling Heath's cup. She leaned her hip against the side of the upholstered booth, and whispered, "Couldn't help overhearing y'all. You talking about the couple from Louisiana?"

"Couple?"

She nodded, leaning in to whisper conspiratorially. "They stopped by last night, not long before closing. Asked about a place to stay for a night or two, and I referred them to Edna's. Gotta tell you, something about the husband gave me the willies. His eyes," she gave an exaggerated shiver, "they were cold and dead. Kinda like a shark, only he seemed so ordinary. You'd probably pass him on the street and never blink. Unless you looked into his eyes. Then you'd pray he didn't slit your throat."

"Whoa, pretty vivid description, Daisy." Jeb leaned back and stared at her, his eyes wide. Heath didn't blame him. He'd known the pretty, perky waitress ever since she'd come to Shiloh Springs to help run the family business, and her words sent chill bumps spreading across his arms.

"Did they talk much? Mention why they were in Shiloh Springs?"

"No. They barely said anything, except to place their order. The man ordered for them both. Come to think of it, they didn't talk much to each other, either. They ate and left, didn't linger."

Heath tossed some money onto the table and stood, Daisy stepping back out of his way. "Jeb, feel like going and having a chat with our Louisiana friends?"

Jeb's answering grin held a touch of unrestrained glee, like he'd been waiting for Heath to ask. "Sounds good."

"Thanks, Daisy."

"No problem. Give me a shout if you need anything else."

The drive to the only bed and breakfast in town took about ten minutes, and Heath parked beside the car with the Louisiana plates. The silver-colored sedan wouldn't warrant a second look in most cases, but the out of state plates stood out in a small town like Shiloh Springs. A cursory glance through the windows didn't reveal anything out of the ordinary for a couple traveling. A plastic bag sat on the floor of the passenger side, and looked like it held fast food napkins and snack cake wrappers.

He and Jeb headed up the front steps, and Heath couldn't help noticing the place was starting to look the worse for the wear. The paint on the shutters was peeling in spots, and a couple of the boards on the porch had nails popped up. He remembered a couple of summers when he'd been a teen, the church had rounded up volunteers, and they'd helped Miss Edna fix the place up. She was a widow lady who'd lived in Shiloh Springs for as long as he could remember, and inherited the bed and breakfast when her husband passed. He made a mental note to talk to his momma. Might be time to gather the troops and give Miss Edna's place a little sprucing up. The bed and breakfast itself was a grand old place, and with a little elbow grease and spit and polish, would again return to the showplace it had once been.

Opening the front door, he strode through with purpose, Jeb following close behind, and headed for the front desk. Glancing through the open office door behind the polished wooden surface, he spotted Miss Edna seated in an over-stuffed chair with her feet propped up on a footrest. Not wanting to make her come to him, he skirted around the reception desk and walked through the office doorway.

"Heath Boudreau, is that you?" Her booming voice echoed through the tiny office space, and he grinned. He'd forgotten Miss Edna's frail appearance might fool you into thinking she was old and delicate, but when she opened her mouth, a longshoreman's voice came out.

"It sure is, Miss Edna. How's my favorite gal?"

Laying her book on her lap, she fluffed her hair, a soft pink blush staining her cheeks. "I'm hanging in there. I haven't seen you in forever. Have you finally stopped all your foolishness and come home?"

"I'm only visiting this time, Miss Edna. I needed to talk to a couple of your guests, so I headed over. I get the added bonus of seeing your beautiful face."

"You always were a flatterer." Dropping her feet off the footrest, she stood. Heath's hand gently cupped her elbow, giving her support as she swayed for a second. Because she was a Shiloh Springs institution, he sometimes forgot she was older than she looked.

"Which one of my guests are you look for?"

"A couple who checked in yesterday. From Louisiana."

Edna nodded, and headed for the reception desk. "You're talking about the Shacklefords. Nice enough folks. They're only staying for the night and are leaving this morning."

"Good thing we got here early then."

She glanced past him, to where Jeb stood. "See you brought a copper with you. Should I be worried?"

Heath's shoulders shook with suppressed laughter at her

old-fashioned term, but he quickly assured her there wasn't anything wrong. Not yet, anyway. If the Shacklefords turned out to be after Camilla, things might degenerate rapidly. Nobody was getting to his girl. Nobody.

He turned at the sound of footsteps on the stairs from the first floor, and spotted a man and woman coming down. Tall and lean, with longish hair the color of tar and eyes to match, Heath instantly realized this was the man Daisy described. His expression held a somber look, though his gaze took in everything around him, finally meeting Heath's intent stare. An almost subtle stiffening of his body caused his step to falter before he resumed his pace down the stairs.

A step or two behind a young woman followed, obviously several years younger than her companion. Her eyes were red-rimmed, evidence she'd been crying. The blouse and jeans she wore appeared to have been slept in, wrinkled and disheveled.

Heath stood at the bottom of the stairs and held out his hand. "Mr. Shackleford?"

"Yeah?"

"My name's Heath Boudreau. I've got a few questions, if you and your companion don't mind."

Shackleford's gaze shot to Jeb, taking in the uniform and the weapon on his hip. "What's this about?" His posture shifted, becoming defensive, and his hand unconsciously blocking the girl from advancing. It almost looked like he was protecting her, raising Heath's curiosity.

"The car you're driving has Louisiana plates, correct?"

Shackleford's brow furrowed. "Yes, why?"

"Did you know that car has been reported stolen?"

"Oh, no!" This from the girl standing behind him. Heath wondered why she looked so panicked at the news.

"Sorry, I have no clue why it would be reported stolen. My cousin loaned us the car."

Jeb pulled a notebook from his pocket. "What's the cousin's name, sir?"

Shackleford gave him a name, and Jeb nodded to Heath. "The last name matches the people who reported the vehicle stolen."

"Why'd you need to borrow a car, Mr. Shackleford?"

He shot a worried glance to the woman. "Gail?"

"It's my fault! We were supposed to take my car, but it broke down. We needed to leave right away. I borrowed Ronny's car, so we could get out of Louisiana." Tears began streaking down the woman's cheeks, and Heath took a better look at her. Shoot, she was barely more than a teenager.

"Why'd you need to leave Louisiana? Did something happen?" The sensation in his gut told him these two didn't have anything to do with Camilla or her shooting. If he had to guess, he'd say the girl was knocked up and they'd run away, eloping, to get away from parents who didn't approve of her choice of baby daddy.

"How is this your business?" Shackleford folded his arms across his chest, his dark-eyed gaze boring into Heath with an intensity that sent chills down his spine. The guy looked to be in his mid to late twenties, far too old to be hanging with a barely legal girl, but this dude gave off a worrisome vibe. Too bad he couldn't arrest somebody simply because of a lousy first impression. So far, he hadn't done anything illegal—at least that he knew about.

"Because of the stolen car, Mr. Shackleford, you've gotten mixed up in the middle of an attempted murder investigation."

"Murder?" Heath watched Shackleford swallow, his Adam's apple bobbing. 'Gail and I don't know anything about a murder! Look, things were lousy for her at home, so we decided to leave. That's it."

"Why'd you pick Shiloh Springs? We're not exactly a top tourist destination or the place runaways head to as their first choice." Jeb's shoulder bumped Heath's after he asked the question. He'd obviously come to the same conclusion Heath had: these idiots weren't the people after Camilla.

Shackleford shrugged, his face turning red. "I got too tired to keep driving. We pulled off the interstate and ended up here. This place is in the middle of nowhere. I didn't think we'd draw any attention, stopping for one night."

"Guess you shouldn't be driving a stolen car then." Heath turned to Jeb. "Check with the people who reported the car stolen and see how they want to handle things."

"You got it." Jeb walked several feet away and pulled out his cell.

"I'm afraid you're going to have to stick around for a little longer until we can get things settled regarding the car. You'd better hope they don't want to press charges."

Heath had forgotten about Miss Edna standing over by the reception desk until she walked across and hooked her arm through Gail's, her hand patting the other girl's arm softly.

"Why don't we head to the kitchen, and I'll make you and your fella some breakfast. Don't worry, Heath's good people, he'll get to the bottom of this in no time."

Heath watched them walk away, a bemused expression on the younger girl's face. A smile tugged at his lips, but he quashed it, hoping Shackleford hadn't noticed. Jeb hung up the phone and walked back over.

"The owner is willing to let things slide if Mr. Shackleford delivers the car back to him by the end of the day—undamaged."

Heath's hand came down hard on Shackleford's shoulder, and he quipped, "Looks like it is your lucky day. You can easily make it to New Orleans by tonight. And keep your nose clean. I'll ask my uncle to check in with you in a couple of weeks, make sure things are going okay with you and Gail."

"Your uncle?"

Heath grinned a shark grin, making sure to put the fear of getting caught into the younger man. "Yeah. You might've heard of him. Gator Boudreau."

All the blood rushed from Shackleford's face, and he audibly gulped. "Guh...Gator Boudreau?"

"Uh-huh. I'm sure he won't mind checking in, making sure everything's copacetic."

"Are we done here? I—we need to get on the road." Shackleford picked up the bag he'd set down earlier and yelled toward the kitchen. "Gail, we don't have time for breakfast, we've gotta leave *now*."

Heath almost felt bad about scaring the dude, but figured the girl's parents were probably worried sick. A little judicious threat might set them on the right path by the time they got back to New Orleans.

Gail sprinted through the opening from the kitchen, and within a minute they'd taken care of their bill and were in their car headed home. Miss Edna turned to face Heath, a huge grin on her wrinkled face.

"Well, that was fun."

"Always a pleasure providing entertainment, Miss Edna."

"Miss Edna," Jeb took a step forward and touched her arm. "There was another car in the parking lot this morning, a rental from Houston. Did they check out?"

"Oh, dear, they left about fifteen minutes before y'all got here. Did you need to talk to them, too?"

"Can you give their contact information to Jeb, Miss Edna? I'll get in touch with them later." He bent down and brushed a light kiss against her cheek, his mind already focusing on Camilla. Too bad this tip hadn't panned out. It would've been nice to take out some of his aggression on somebody.

"Sorry things didn't work out, buddy. I'll keep looking." Jeb clapped him on the shoulder and headed down the front porch steps.

Frustrated, Heath followed, softly cursing the lousy turn of events, and wondering if he'd ever find the threat to Camilla.

CHAPTER EIGHTEEN

"Hello?"

"Is this Camilla Stewart?"

Camilla hesitated a second before responding. "Yes. How can I help you?"

"Ms. Stewart, this is Destiny. I work for Ridge Boudreau. I'm the resident computer specialist."

Camilla let out the breath she'd been holding. She wasn't sure why she'd anticipated bad news when she answered the phone. "Of course. Heath mentioned you were going to work on my cell phone, see if you could figure out if there was anything on it that might hold a clue to why somebody's after me."

"Exactly. I downloaded everything onto my computer, and I've got a couple of things I'd like to discuss with you and Mr. Boudreau."

"That's great. Heath's in town right now, but he should be back soon. Do you want us to meet you someplace?"

"Might be better if I met you, Ms. Stewart. You're at the Big House, right? I've got a few of things to take care of this morning, but I should be able to get there in a couple of hours. Does that work for you?"

"We'll be here. I'll text Heath as soon as we're done here and let him know you're coming." Her fingers tapped on the kitchen table, and she hesitated for a minute before asking, "Can you give me a clue what you've found? I want my life back."

"In this case, Ms. Stewart, seeing is believing. I think you're going to be surprised at what I've found. We are talking shock and awe here. Shock. And. Awe." Destiny's cheerful voice helped alleviate at least a modicum of the fear roiling in Camilla's gut. It couldn't be all bad if she sounded so freaking happy about things, right?

"Okay. See you in a couple hours."

She hung up and stared down at her nearly empty plate. Somehow, she'd managed to sleep later than normal this morning, and then lingered over breakfast, thinking about the scene she'd worked on before deciding to get something to eat. Ever since she'd been shot, her writing schedule had been turned topsy-turvy, and the deadline had flown out the window. Chances were good she'd have to ask for an extension on said deadline, something she hated doing, because it meant disappointing her fans.

Taking a deep breath, she sent a text to Heath, telling him about Destiny's call and that she wanted to meet with them in a couple hours. Then she rinsed her breakfast dishes, put them into the dishwasher, and poured another cup of coffee. She always joked with Beth that she didn't have red blood cells, she had caffeine running through her veins.

Heading to the living room of the Big House, she quickly settled into the large cushy chair she'd confiscated as her temporary writing spot. She'd already turned on her laptop before she'd sat down to breakfast, and now she pulled up her e-mails, scrolling through to see if there was anything needing immediate attention. One in particular caught her eye and she clicked the icon to open it.

Her eyes widened at the brief note from the police department in North Carolina. Reading through it, she bit back a laugh. Officer Dandridge asked if she knew Etienne Boudreau, also known as Gator. Apparently, he was asking some pointed questions of the good detective and giving him grief about things he'd missed in his investigation.

Sounded like Officer Dandridge wasn't too happy with having a second set of eyes peering over his shoulder. Too bad. Knowing Heath's Uncle Gator had turned his focus onto finding out who'd shot at her made Camilla feel better. At least he cared enough to take a personal interest. Douglas and Heath had both assured her if anybody could get to the bottom of who was after Camilla, it was Gator. She believed them.

She shot an e-mail back to the policeman, assuring him Gator Boudreau was investigating her case, and had authorization to see all records pertaining to the police's investigation. While she was at it, she also asked for an update on what progress had been made in catching her shooter.

When her text alert dinged, she read Heath's response. He'd try and be back by the time Destiny got there, but he might be a little late. *Wonder what he's sticking his nose into today? I swear, the man is a danger magnet.*

With e-mail out of the way, she pulled up her manuscript and read through the last scene she'd written, getting her head back into the story. Heat began to flood her cheeks when she realized the hero of this book had somehow morphed into Heath. Mortified, she closed her eyes and rested her face in her palms. She never used real people in her books. Oh, sure, she might take a characteristic from somebody once in a while, but nothing obvious. Yet staring at the words on the laptop screen, anybody who knew Heath in real life would instantly recognize Detective Shane McBride as a doppelgänger for the real thing. Making a note to go back and make changes, she focused on the story of the hunky detective helping lead the search for the kidnapped bank vice president with the help of the sexy private investigator who portrayed the love interest.

Suddenly the words flowed from her brain like watching a high-definition movie, technicolor with scenes and dialogue making the story come alive. It was awesome when that happened, because it didn't all the time. Some days it was a struggle to get ten words written. Today, it felt like the book wrote itself. It was blessedly quiet, everybody either out working the ranch, or headed toward their day jobs. Nica had gone with Ms. Patti to the real estate office, and the relative silence allowed her to concentrate on the words flowing effortlessly. She knew somebody was around; Heath would have made sure of that. He never let her out of his sight unless one of his brothers or his parents could watch over her.

A knock on the front door snapped her out of her writing bubble, and she glanced at the clock in the corner of her screen. Three hours since she'd sat down to write. Walking to the front door, she spotted a woman standing on the front porch, her dark hair cut in a short pixie style. She must have heard or spotted Camilla, because she smiled and waved.

When she opened the door, the woman held out her hand. "I'm Destiny, computer genius extraordinaire." She hitched her messenger bag strap higher on her shoulder. A hint of a tattoo peeked out above the edge of her black tank top. Camilla couldn't make out what it was, but the vivid colors intrigued her. Her writer's brain made her immediately realize none of the women she'd written about had tattoos, and she made a mental note to write a female character with tattoos. The petite brunette tucked a strand of hair behind her ear, with a casualness that felt genuine and Camilla's instincts immediately trusted the quirky brunette.

"Hi. Camilla Stewart. Come on in. We've got a few minutes, Heath's not here yet."

"Great."

"Give me a sec to save what I'm working on," Camilla

said, heading for her laptop. Even with auto save, she always saved her books to multiple places, including onto the cloud and on thumb drives, as well as e-mailing it to herself. She'd learned the hard way you could never have enough backed up data. Having to recreate an entire book because the original file got corrupted was something she never wanted to repeat.

"Can I get you something to drink?"

"Tea would be great."

"I think Ms. Patti left a pitcher of sweet tea in the fridge."

Destiny grinned. "Sweet tea. It's a southern thing. I'd never heard of it before I moved to Texas. Now I'm addicted to the stuff, though my hips aren't too happy with me."

"I've had it all my life, but then I'm from Charlotte. It's normal there."

"California."

Camilla poured two glasses of sweet tea and gestured toward the kitchen table. Destiny looped her messenger bag over the back of the chair and sat, taking a long drink of the tea.

"Thanks, I needed that. I've been up most of the night, working on deciphering your phone."

"Care to give me a hint what you found? I know you want to wait until Heath gets here, but the suspense is killing me."

"I noticed you've got a ton of photos on there. Buildings,

places, people. Good thing you've got a lot of memory."

Camilla nodded as Destiny spoke. "That's true. I'm a writer, so I'm constantly looking for things that fit the book I'm writing or for future books. It might be a corner of a building or a sign. Maybe a fountain. Or a person, who fits the image of somebody in the story." She stopped for a moment, remembering New Orleans. "That's how my phone got confiscated in the first place. We'd gone out to dinner in New Orleans, and I'd never been there. I turned on the phone and started snapping pictures. Heath nearly had a conniption fit when he saw what I'd done."

"He's right. GPS on phones can be tracked by almost anybody. Wives looking for cheating husbands. Businesses trailing their employees to make sure they're on the job when they're supposed to be. It's as easy as downloading an app."

Camilla stood and began pacing. She needed something to do, because she felt like she'd been confined in a box for weeks. Everybody and everything around her was guided by somebody else. Her memories still hadn't returned, other than the little bits and pieces she'd garnered the day she, Nica, and Beth tried the meditation exercises. She wondered if she'd ever get them back.

"I'm sorry. Everything's closing in around me and I feel like my life's spinning out of control. I got shot. Almost attacked by a rattlesnake. Forced to leave my home and traipse halfway across the country because somebody decided my life didn't matter. I have a gap in my memory because of this stupid amnesia, and I want this over. I want to know who's playing with my life like a bloody puppet master, pulling the strings and making me dance to his tune. I hate this. I want my life back."

"You'll get it back, Cam. I promise."

She spun around at the sound of Heath's voice, her hand on her chest. "Heath, you scared me."

"Sorry, darlin'." He walked into the kitchen and held out his hand. "You must be Destiny."

"I am. Nice to meet you, Mr. Boudreau."

"Make it Heath." He went to Camilla, wrapping his arms around her from behind and pulling her close against his chest. Closing her eyes, she leaned against him, feeling the comfort and warmth exuding from him.

"I was telling Camilla I downloaded the contents of her phone onto my computer, and I've combed through everything. Checked all her incoming and outgoing calls. Text messages. Apps. Photos. Everything on that phone's been gone over with a fine-tooth comb."

"And?"

"I found something unexpected." Destiny pulled her messenger bag onto her lap and pulled out her computer, placing it on the kitchen table. "I might be totally out in left field with this, you know?"

"Whatever it is, I need to know. I can't imagine what might be on my phone that would lead somebody to try and kill me, so anything you've found might give me a clue to figuring it out."

Heath's phone rang, and he reached into his pocket, and stared at the caller ID. "Sorry, I've got to take this." He glanced at Camilla, and added, "It's Gator."

A tingle of excitement raced through her at Gator's name. From everything she'd heard about the man since getting to Shiloh Springs, she'd convinced herself that he'd be the one to find answers. Maybe…maybe he'd solved the mystery of her shooter.

"Go ahead. Put it on speaker."

Heath shot a glance at Destiny, who shrugged. "I can leave the room."

"No, it's okay. You're working the case, you might as well hear." He swiped to answer. "Hey, Uncle Gator."

"Boy, don't you ever answer your phone?" Gator's Cajun accent came through loud and clear.

"Sorry, I was questioning some folks from Louisiana, following up on a lead. Unfortunately, it didn't pan out."

"I e-mailed you something. Want you and Camilla to take a good look at it. I have the feeling this is the final piece of the puzzle, and I'll explain everything after you've seen the photos. Call me back."

The line went dead. Camilla's eyes met Heath's, and he shrugged. "He's not much for small talk."

"You want to look at his stuff first, or do you want to see what I found?"

"Let's do both. You show Camilla what you found and

I'm going to check Gator's e-mail. See what he sent. Maybe we'll compare notes."

"Works for me." Destiny hooked her ankle around the empty chair and pulled it closer, motioning Camilla to sit. Within seconds, she was typing on the laptop, and Camilla blinked at the speed of her flying fingers. Personally, she typed about a hundred words a minute, but Destiny? The woman's hands flew across the keyboard, only pausing long enough to manipulate the mouse.

"Alright. I went through the photos on your phone. Probably ninety to ninety-five percent of them were places and stuff. Honestly, there wasn't much there that grabbed my attention, so I figured I'd look at the ones that had people in them. Basically, places and things are static, stationary. They don't change much. People on the other hand, they are fluid. They constantly change. Gain weight, lose weight. Change the color of their hair. Grow facial hair or shave it all off. Now, taking into account you aren't a paparazzi taking pics of celebrities or famous people, I played a hunch."

"What kind of hunch?"

Destiny pulled up a screen showing about two dozen thumbnail-sized photos Camilla recognized. Some were of Beth, Jamie, and Tessa. One of Nica and Ms. Patti. There were also her parents and a single photo of her brother, Evan. She'd forgotten that one. Another couple of shots were of her neighbors and the maintenance man who cared for the yard around her townhouse. A couple were of a woman she'd spotted who resembled the heroine from her last book, and she'd asked if she could take the pics. One little boy she'd seen at the local ice cream parlor who had the cutest chocolate mustache. There was even a shot of her neighbor's dog, who'd been doing a dance and standing on his back legs. It had been adorable, and she'd snuck the picture when Mr. Davis wasn't looking.

"I ran the faces through a facial recognition program I use for my investigative work. Buddy of mine developed it a few years back, and I helped do some tweaking on it. The program's good enough the government uses it. It's precise, far better than most of them out there."

Camilla felt ready to explode. Destiny kept droning on and on when all she wanted was answers.

"Destiny, what did you find?" Her frustration must have bled into her voice, because the other woman winced slightly.

"Sorry. I tend to get carried away with the minutia and forget others couldn't care less about how I found something. They want answers." She brushed her dark hair behind one ear, and then pointed to the picture of Mr. Davis' puppy.

"That's Oscar. Yeah, I know, not an original name, but my neighbor's not really creative."

"Your neighbor?" Destiny choked on the words, then took a long swallow of her tea.

"Yes, Mr. Davis. Oscar's his Yorkie. I always stop and give him a scratch when he's outside and I'm checking the mail. Why?"

"How much do you know about your neighbor?"

The bottom dropped out of Camilla's stomach. He'd moved into the townhouse beside hers about six months earlier. Mostly kept to himself, other than the occasional hello when they passed on the way out. Thinking about it, when he'd caught up with her leaving the hospital was probably the longest conversation they'd had.

"I need to know the answer to that question too, Cam." Heath walked back into the kitchen, his eyes wide, his skin a little pale.

"Okay, what's going on? Why are you asking about Mr. Davis?"

Heath met Destiny's eyes, and she shrugged and pointed to the picture of Davis and his dog. His face was mostly in profile, but enough showed he was clearly identifiable.

"Mr. Davis? What can you tell me about him?"

"Not a lot to tell." Camilla shrugged and stared at the photo. "He moved next door about six months ago. Nice enough, though we're not chummy. I've probably spent more time with his dog than with him, to be honest. Why?"

"I don't know about the name Davis, but my facial recognition identified him as Johnny Grimaldi." Destiny hesitated a beat or two, and Camilla had the feeling she was waiting for Camilla to recognize the name or something.

Too bad, because it didn't ring any bells.

"Sorry, the name means nothing to me."

"You've never heard of Johnny 'The Chain' Grimaldi? Capo of the Grimaldi crime family? Girl, don't you read the news? The man's been all over the papers in the last year. The feds have been looking for him on charges of extortion, racketeering, and he's suspected of half a dozen murders in New Jersey and Pennsylvania." She tapped the picture on the screen. "Of course, this man doesn't resemble the news photos. Hair's been dyed gray. The mustache and beard are new, too. He also looks about twenty years older than his mid-forties, which is his actual age. Wonder if he's using makeup to age his features. The cane's a nice touch too, because he's known to have taken a bullet to the knee. Allegedly the slug's still in there."

"Your program must be wrong. I mean, you can't even see his face. Mr. Davis is a nice old man. Doesn't have any family—"

She broke off at Destiny's snicker. "He's got family alright. He's connected to one of the biggest Mafioso families on the Eastern seaboard. This guy is on every government agency watchlist. Catching him would be a coup for whichever one manages to capture him. Nobody would except him to be holed up in a townhouse in North Carolina."

"Cam, she's right."

Camilla turned her gaze to Heath's, her mind whizzing

in a thousand directions. None of this made sense. How was it possible her next-door neighbor wasn't the kindly old man she knew? A monster, connected to the mob, and worst of all—a killer?

"Let's say Mr. Davis is who you say, this Johnny 'The Chain' Grimaldi. Why would he want to kill me? It doesn't make any sense."

"Gator's been watching him for the last couple of days. He's been investigating the complex, and he staked out your place. He did a thorough sweep of your townhouse and found signs somebody'd been there after we left. Place had been trashed. Decided he'd keep an eye on the townhouse, see if somebody came back. The minute he spotted your neighbor, William Davis, alarm bells went off in his brain."

"Who's Gator?" Camilla started at Destiny's voice. She'd almost forgotten the other woman was in the room, focused on Heath's intense stare.

"Gator Boudreau, my uncle. He does some private investigative work." Heath grinned, and continued, "I can neither confirm nor deny that he's former military intelligence and has worked for The Agency."

Destiny's eyes widened at his words. "Oooh, he's a spook? That's so cool." Camilla could almost hear the wheels turning in her brain. "Do you think I could meet him?"

Heath's laugh was infectious, and Camilla found herself joining in. "Stick around the Boudreaus long enough, you'll get the chance. He and his family have a standing invitation to Thanksgiving and Christmas."

"Awesome." The light in Destiny's eyes gleamed like a zealot viewing their messiah.

"Guys, can we get back to my neighbor?"

Heath squatted down beside Camilla, taking her hands between his. "Cam, darlin', when did you take his picture?"

She struggled to remember when the photo was taken. Remembered it had been on a Saturday, because she'd been coming home from her grocery run, and had her takeout lunch in one hand and her phone in the other, reading a text message from her mother. Oscar raced up to the fence as she walked past, barking and jumping at Camilla, and Mr. Davis had limped forward toward the gate, trying to bribe him with a treat, while Oscar danced on his back legs. The moment's sweetness had her snapping the picture on impulse.

"The photo's metadata shows it was taken at 12:42 on Saturday, October fourth."

"Did Davis know you took the picture, Cam?"

She shook her head vehemently. "No. I started to show him, because Oscar looked cute, and I thought he might like a copy. Then I remembered when I'd taken his picture once before, he made me delete it. Said something about hating to have his photo taken, so I didn't mention it."

"Makes sense. Nobody's seen or heard a peep about Grimaldi for almost ten months. He disappeared without a trace."

"Probably because he disappeared with a fortune in diamonds. Scuttlebutt has it he planned to skip the country, using the stones to have a cushy lifestyle in a nonextradition country. I can't figure out why he's still in the U.S. Not with the government searching high and low for him, not to mention the Family. They aren't happy he skipped with millions of dollars of their money, which he allegedly converted into the diamonds I mentioned." Reaching up, he gently pushed a lock of hair behind her ear, a curiously gentle smile on his face. "I'm not sure how, but he must've somehow figured out you'd took the picture."

Heath stood and ran a hand through his hair, leaving it mussed, and Camilla bit back her smile. Even with the seriousness of the situation, she couldn't help thinking he looked adorable.

"Bet he wanted to get his hands on your phone. That'd be the only way to be sure the photo wasn't made public. Steal your phone, delete it from the cloud and from the physical device. And your computer. Ta da, the evidence is gone. Oh, boy. I told you, girlfriend. Shock and awe!" Destiny grinned and closed her laptop. "I love my job."

"But it's only one picture and it's not even showing his whole face. It's hard to say with one hundred percent certainty it's this mobster."

"Not anymore." Heath handed his phone to Camilla, and she saw a full-faced photo of William Davis. "Gator took several and e-mailed them to me. He's sure it's

Grimaldi, even with the changes in his appearance."

She scrolled through the photos Gator sent, staring at the face of the man she thought she knew. He was good, she had to admit. She'd never suspected he wasn't exactly who he'd claimed to be, a retired insurance salesman who wanted to live out his golden years in peace and quiet. What a crock!

"He shot me?"

"Gator suspects Grimaldi simply wanted to get access to your phone. Using a gun isn't his usual M.O. Probably expected to use the chaos and confusion of the police and ambulance dealing with the scene. Nobody would notice if he picked up your phone and pocketed it. And if they did, he could simply say he was being neighborly and taking care of it for you. It's actually not a bad scenario."

Camilla raised her hand to stop him. "But he didn't have my phone."

"Something must have happened, and he wasn't able to get it. Maybe the cops or an EMT picked it up. It was with your stuff at the hospital." Heath cupped her cheek, his thumb brushing against her skin in a soft caress.

"I wonder if that's why he came to see me at the hospital?"

"What?" Heath's eyes narrowed, his gaze accusatory. "You never mentioned he came to see you."

"Honestly, with everything going on, I forgot. I ran into him in the lobby when you went to get the car. We talked for a few minutes. I haven't seen him since."

"Well, folks, as fascinating as this is, I think you've got a lot to talk about, so I'm gonna hit the bricks. Heath, can you e-mail me a copy of the photos Gator sent you? Might be best to have a backup nobody knows about. Just in case, you know?"

"Good idea. Thanks for all your help, Destiny."

"Looks like you'd have figured it out without me, but I've got to admit, it's been a blast. I've never got to dig into a serial killer before, much less somebody like The Chain."

"Alright, I'm dying to know. Why do they call him *The Chain*?" Camilla's gaze darted between Destiny and Heath, wondering if either one of them would answer her question. Heath wanted to keep her wrapped in cottonwool, and she was tired of being treated like she only had half a brain. She'd have to remind him she wasn't meek or weak.

"Johnny Grimaldi's signature killing style is to strangle his victims. Then he wraps a gold chain about their throat. It's kind of his trademark." Destiny glanced at Heath, as if asking permission to say more.

"Don't look at him, he doesn't answer for me." Camilla's voice hardened, and she spat out, "Tell me."

Destiny took a deep breath, like she was bracing herself to impart bad news. "The Chain's victims have all been women. Usually former lovers or women who've betrayed him." She paused and Camilla read between the lines what she wasn't saying.

"He'll consider my taking his picture a betrayal." A

shudder wracked her body, and she swallowed the bile that rose to the back of her throat. "That's why he wants me dead."

"Sorry, but yeah, that's what I'm thinking." Destiny glanced at Heath again. "If I were you, I'd set up extra surveillance on Camilla."

"Already got it covered."

"I'm out of here. Call me if you need anything."

After she left, Heath slid onto the chair beside Camilla and tilted her face up, brushing a soft kiss against her lips. She responded, letting the sweetness of his kiss wash over her, obliterating the awful truth she'd just heard.

Slowly breaking the kiss, she studied his face, reading the steadfastness and determination in his tense jaw and steely eyes. With everything she now knew, it was time to stop running and take the fight home. Taking a deep breath, she spoke.

"Looks like things aren't over yet. But I've got a plan."

CHAPTER NINETEEN

Camilla's silence throughout the flight had Heath's teeth on edge. Oh, she'd answered him if he asked her something. Otherwise she'd stayed inside her head, and it was driving him insane. After she claimed to have a plan, she'd made plane reservations to fly to Charlotte. He had the feeling the only reason he sat by her side on the flight was because he'd insisted.

"Ever going to tell me what your plan is? Because I've gotta say, you're starting to scare me with your silence."

She blinked, her gaze darting toward his, before ducking her head with a chagrined grimace. "Sorry. I didn't mean to shut you out; I've been making a mental list of what I'm going to need.

"Such as? Sweetheart, I can help. I need to make sure Grimaldi doesn't get another chance to hurt you. It's eating me up inside, knowing you've been living beside a serial killer and nobody had a clue."

"Trust me, Heath, I'm having trouble wrapping my head around the facts myself. Mr. Davis, I mean Mr. Grimaldi, seemed like a normal old guy. A little reclusive, but I chalked that up to him being a lifelong bachelor. Makes me wonder if I have the sense the Good Lord gave a goose, because I should have known he was up to something."

Heath grabbed the hand she waved around as she spoke and brushed a soft kiss against her palm. "I doubt anybody would have seen through the persona he showed the public. Remember, he was in hiding. The cops, the Feds, everybody was searching high and low for Grimaldi. What better disguise than somebody decades older than his actual age, living a quiet, secluded life in the burbs?" Heath shifted in his seat, facing toward her. "How about clueing me in on what you're planning? I'll help with anything you need."

Camilla leaned her head back against the headrest, chewing on her bottom lip. Her eyes held an almost frantic gleam, one that scared him a little. Knowing her, she'd plunge headfirst into danger without a second thought, if it meant putting Grimaldi behind bars. He didn't have a problem with that notion, as long as she wasn't in danger. Might be a bit of an issue, because he doubted Grimaldi would go along with the cops peacefully.

"Gator's watching Grimaldi's place still, right?"

Heath nodded. "He is."

"Okay. What about the police or the government? Has anybody told them Grimaldi's been located?"

"As far as I know, no. I wanted him turned in, but Gator wanted to wait. His gut is telling him something big is about to blow. I trust his instincts; they've never been wrong."

"That works for me."

"Why? He shot you, sweetheart. I'd think you'd want him behind bars, where he can't hurt anybody ever again."

The smile on Camilla's lips was vicious, one he'd never seen on her beautiful lips before. It scared him because he couldn't read her intentions. She had a plan, she'd admitted as much, but for the life of him, he couldn't figure out what she was up to.

"We need to make a couple of stops on the way to my place."

"Nope." Heath folded his arms across his chest. He wasn't allowing her anywhere near her townhouse, not as long as Grimaldi was free and next door. Nuh-uh, not happening.

Camilla's laughter sounded like the sweetest music. "Poor baby, it's driving you crazy, not knowing what I've got in store for Grimaldi, isn't it?"

"Yes. I don't like walking into this blind. Too many things can go wrong. We know he's got at least one gun, and I figure he's got a whole lot more. Grimaldi isn't the kind to allow himself to be vulnerable. Chances are good he's got an arsenal in his place. You're not safe going back to your home."

"The only way this works is if I surprise him. He's not going to expect me to walk into my place. Especially alone."

"Cam—"

"Just listen. You and Gator will be right outside. Call in

the cavalry, but nobody's going to believe he's the person who shot me. Not without proof. I can get that proof. He doesn't know his real identity has been exposed, so he's feeling safe. As far as he knows, I've been out of town for a couple days and now I'm back. My memories are gone, so he's in the clear."

Heath shook his head vehemently. "He'll never buy it. Cam, he ran one of the major mafia families on the East Coast. The minute you walk through the door to your townhouse, he's going to contact a hitman to take you out. You'll never see it coming."

"I'm not giving him time to call anybody. I drop off my suitcase, and head over to Grimaldi's place. I'll wear a wire. I can make him believe I've got my memories back. I'll tell him I know who shot me and get him to admit it. You and Gator, and anybody else you want, can be right outside. The minute he incriminates himself, he's toast."

He banged his head several times against the headrest, wondering when Camilla had lost her mind. Because nobody with a brain in their head could possibly think this hair-brained scheme would work.

"You're kidding. Please tell me you're joking. Pretty girl, as much as I love you, there's no power on earth that's letting you walk into Grimaldi's townhouse alone."

At Camilla's startled gasp, he realized what he'd said. He hadn't meant to blurt his feelings out like that. No, he wanted something romantic. Candlelit dinner for two, dancing to soft music, and kisses under the stars. Not throwing it out there in the middle of a disagreement. *Smooth, Boudreau, smooth. You're a real piece of work. Can't even tell the woman you love how you feel without screwing it up.*

"Heath? You love me?"

He gave her a lopsided grin. "Yeah. Wasn't quite the way I'd planned on saying it the first time, but—"

"I love you, too!" Her hands flew to her mouth, and the prettiest blush stained her cheeks.

"You do?"

"Of course I do. I think I've been in love with you from the first time I saw you all those months ago."

"Even though I was an obnoxious jerk?"

"How could I not love you? You brought me alive with your teasing and taunting and overall horrible behavior. You infuriated me and befuddled me, and I couldn't stop thinking about you. Believe me, I tried."

He chuckled and flung his arm around her shoulder, pulling her close against him. Or as close as airline seats would allow, which wasn't nearly enough. When she relaxed against him, he closed his eyes, unable to believe the woman he adored loved him back.

"I want to kiss you, but I'm afraid if I start, I'll never be able to stop," he confessed.

"Hold that thought, Goober. I plan to kiss you too, but not until we're firmly on the ground. For now, let's figure out how we're going to get Grimaldi out of my life once and for all.

Camilla sat quietly, watching Heath and Officer Dandridge quietly argue, neither giving any ground. They'd headed from the airport straight to the police station. Heath refused to let her head home, proclaiming they needed to bring the police in on her "brilliant" plan. He'd laid on the sarcasm, but her gut told her they were on the right track. Grimaldi wouldn't be able to resist doing the whole villain soliloquy once he realized Camilla had discovered his identity and knew he'd been the one to shoot her.

Heath called his Uncle Gator as soon as they'd touched down, even before they'd left the airport, explaining the plan to set a trap for Grimaldi. He'd talked in a hushed whisper, and she'd tuned him out, making her own plans for when she confronted him. No way was she letting Heath or his uncle talk her out of it. She was reclaiming her life.

Letting Grimaldi think she'd gotten her memories back seemed the perfect opening salvo. Oh, she wouldn't open with that information; she'd need to be subtle. Make him believe she'd simply gone away for a few days to recover. He'd probably offer some phony sympathy, and she'd play along, encourage him in believing he'd gotten away with the attempt on her life.

"Ms. Stewart, please reconsider." Dandridge leaned on the table between them and stared at her. "You're placing yourself in an untenable situation, one I cannot condone or approve."

"I'm not asking for your approval, Officer Dandridge. I'm giving you the opportunity to be on scene when I meet with Mr. Grimaldi. Giving you a chance to help coordinate the capture of a wanted criminal, one who's being hunted by the police, the Feds, and who knows who else wants a piece of him."

Dandridge straightened, shaking his head. "I've got to bring my captain in on this before you pull this harebrained stunt. He's gonna blow a gasket, if he doesn't toss both of your butts in a cell."

"Wouldn't you rather get credit for the bust? I bet you don't want the Feds stealing all the glory."

He rolled his eyes. "You've been watching too much TV. I don't care who gets the credit. Getting Grimaldi off the streets and into custody is what matters." He shot her a heated stare. "Of course, keeping you from getting your head blown off sounds like a good plan. You realize if this goes south, Grimaldi's going to be screaming about entrapment, false arrest, and anything else he can come up with?

Camilla gave him one of her sweetest smiles and patted his hand. "Which is why I came here before we put our plan into effect. I want to do this right."

Dandridge shook his head. "Let me go get the captain."

Heath walked over, pulled her to her feet and wrapped his arms around her. Closing her eyes, she leaned against him, willing her body to relax. She'd put up a good front for Dandridge, unwilling to admit she was terrified. But she knew this was a good plan.

"You okay?"

"Yes. I wish people understood this will work."

"Because you're basing how you think Grimaldi's going to react based on the six months you've known him. The cops are looking at his record, at the number of people he's suspected of killing. It's their job to keep you safe, even from yourself."

"That's why we came here first. I don't want to walk into this without weighing all the options, knowing the risks and benefits. I want all the safeguards in place. I'm not a fool."

Heath's arms tightened around her, and she felt the tiny tremor of his body against hers. "If Grimaldi suspects anything, we're screwed."

"Heath, I'm doing this to avoid any bloodshed. If the SWAT team or the Feds surround his townhouse, there's a chance people are going to die. This way, there's a good chance to keep anybody from being hurt or killed."

"Except you. Babe, he's already tried to kill you once. What's to stop him from doing it again?"

Before she could answer, Dandridge was back with a barrel-chested, graying man who nearly matched Heath in height. From the scowl on his face, and the aura of command, she guessed he must be the police captain.

"You're Camilla Stewart?" His gruff-sounding voice sound like he chewed rocks in his free time, the low rumble meant to be intimidating. It worked.

"I am."

"How sure are you the next-door neighbor is Grimaldi? I'm not authorizing a dang thing on a hunch."

"Are you familiar with what Johnny Grimaldi looks like?" Heath pulled out his cell phone and keyed up the photos Gator sent him. Camilla stood back and let him deal with the captain. Sure, this was her plan and she'd be the one sticking her neck on the line, but Heath worked for the government. Not trying to paint the captain with a sexist brush, but she figured he'd probably deal better with another person in a position of authority, rather than somebody who wrote romance novels for a living.

"Where'd you get these?"

"Confidential source." She almost grinned at Heath's refusal to give the captain his Uncle Gator's name. There was enough evidence, in addition to the photos; Gator could be protected.

"Is this 'confidential source' reliable? Somebody whose testimony would stand up in court?"

Heath chuckled. "Not a problem, believe me."

The captain pulled out the chair opposite where Camilla had been sitting and motioned for her to sit.

"Tell me exactly what you've got, and about this cocka-mamie stunt you're planning."

Camilla did.

CHAPTER TWENTY

It felt like an alien crawled into her stomach and now fought to climb its way out through her throat. Camilla swallowed and stared at the front door of her townhouse, wondering if she'd lost her mind. Maybe this was all a nightmare and she'd wake up and find she'd dreamed the whole thing. Nobody got shot. A gangster slash murderer wasn't her next-door neighbor. And Heath Boudreau hadn't told her he loved her. Well, she kind of hoped that part wasn't a dream, but the rest of it?

The police arranged for one of their undercover officers to drive her home, making it appear she'd caught a ride from the airport. Heath's rental followed discreetly behind, in case Grimaldi spotted her arrival. She couldn't picture him standing at his front window, peering through the blinds, but why take the chance? Gator Boudreau remained close by, but she didn't try to spot him. No reason to draw unwanted attention to somebody who was helping her out, and she didn't want him any more involved than he already was.

Climbing from the backseat, she grabbed her bag, and thanked the driver, who pulled away. Camilla was sure he'd circle back and park in the lot at a discreet distance, ready to provide support. Pulling out her keys, she unlocked her front door and walked inside. She stopped, taking in the destruction. Chairs were overturned, drawers pulled out and emptied on the floor. Though she'd been expecting it, since Gator told Heath about finding it like this, her body still rocked with shock.

Dropping her bag by the front door, she tossed her purse onto the console table and stepped back outside. The undercover police officers were positioned, having been sent to set up by the captain before she ever left the police station. The only thing left to do was test the mic taped to her body, and the tiny earpiece in her right ear.

"Testing. Can you hear me?"

"Loud and clear, Ms. Stewart," came through the earpiece. "You're good to go."

"Great," she mumbled. Squaring her shoulders, she braced herself, and walked up the pathway leading to Grimaldi's front door. Taking a deep breath, she reached for the doorbell and hesitated.

This is it. Time to put on my big girl panties and catch a killer. Oh, good night, what am I doing? I can't do this. What was I thinking? I'm a writer, not a detective. I'm insane. That's it, I've gone crazy. That's the only excuse I've got. Stark raving, round the bend, lost my mind crazy.

"Camilla, dear, are you alright?"

Holy hotdogs, she wasn't ready. Except she didn't have a

choice now, it was too late.

"Mr. Davis, I...I'm so glad you're home. Can I come in?"

"Of course, of course. Is something wrong?"

Camilla found her eyes trying to take in everything in his townhouse. The place was spotless. Oscar raced to her, yipping and dancing around her feet, standing on his hind legs, overflowing with excitement. Squatting, she petted the cute pup, though she never lost sight of where Grimaldi stood. He seemed cordial enough, she thought, considering the monster tried to kill me.

"I don't know what to do. After I got hurt, a friend of mine came and we went out of town for a bit. I got home, and my place is a wreck. I think somebody broke in while I was gone." Still playing with the dog, she cut her gaze to his face, wanting to watch his expression.

"I didn't realize you'd gone away. How are you doing? All healed up?" He motioned toward the living room when she stood. "I wish I'd known you were out of town. I'd have kept a better eye on your place. It's the neighborly thing to do."

Sitting on the edge of the sofa, her body shuddered with tension. Hopefully, he'd rack it up to the alleged break in at her place, and not the fact she was setting him up to spill the beans. *Relax, you need to get him talking. You're not alone, remember? There are a dozen cops outside. Heath's listening and waiting. Let's get this done, and then we'll be together.*

"I'm healing up nicely according to the doctors. I've been poked and prodded enough to last a lifetime, to say nothing of all the brain scans and MRIs. I think losing my memory was the worst part. Can you imagine somebody taking a shot at you, and not knowing who did it?"

She noticed the tic at the corner of his mouth at her words. The iciness of his stare hardened, and she knew she'd hit a nerve. Time to dig a little deeper.

"I can't imagine not being able to remember something so important."

"That's true. I *had* amnesia surrounding the shooting."

"Had? Does that mean you remember what happened?"

She deliberately leaned back, crossing her legs, and letting her expression harden. "I remember…everything."

A long moment passed, the air rife with unexpressed tension before he finally sighed. "I see. I presume this means we have a problem."

"A bit of an understatement, Mr. Davis." She deliberately crossed her arms over her chest, before adding, "Or should I call you Mr. Grimaldi?"

She almost laughed at his indrawn gasp. He really had no clue she knew his secret identity. *How's he going to handle it?*

"I'm sorry, who?"

Smoothing a hand down her skirt, she studied the hem, letting him stew a bit before she answered.

"Do you really want to play this game? I'm a writer. I'm exceptionally good at doing research, especially when I sense a puzzle. And you're an interesting puzzle. It didn't take long to figure out you were hiding something. Now, imagine my surprise when I connected the dots that led me straight to Johnny 'The Chain' Grimaldi. A little more digging and I found out there's quite a substantial reward for information regarding you, Mr. Grimaldi."

Grimaldi's expression hardened until it looked like it was carved in stone. His eyes, though, those weren't expressionless. Far from it. A shiver raced down Camilla's spine at the hatred and coldness within their depths. Along with a healthy dose of fear. Inside, she was shaking to pieces, though outwardly she struggled at keeping her expression serene and calm. She couldn't afford to blow this. Too much was riding on getting him to admit to shooting her.

"How long have you known?"

She sighed, feigning an exasperated demeanor. "Does it matter? I want to know why you took a shot at me."

"You witch! You really do remember everything."

Camilla reached down to pet Oscar's head. He'd settled at her feet, licking her ankle and trying to get her attention. The pup's desperate need for affection had her wondering how much he got from Grimaldi. Poor baby.

She quirked a brow and chuckled. "I believe I already told you I got my memory back. It was risky, taking a potshot at me, wasn't it? Especially since you had to talk to the cops who came to investigate my shooting. You were smart to play things vague, no specific details. Coming forward and showing sympathy for your poor neighbor. Such a standup citizen. Weren't you worried somebody'd figure out your disguise, recognize you on sight? I'll admit, it's good, by the way. Old man, retired, lives alone, disabled and with a cane. Of course, keeping up with dying your hair gray is probably a pain in the backside."

Grimaldi lowered himself on a chair, wincing when his knee bent. "I'm curious. What gave me away?"

Oops, she hadn't been expecting that question. She wracked her brain, trying to come up with something plausible. "Your paranoia about having your picture taken was my first clue. Remember when I took the pic of you and Oscar? You overreacted to a simple photo, demanding I delete it. Which I did, but it made me wonder."

"And you couldn't resist digging your nose into my business."

She shrugged. "What can I say? I'm naturally curious."

Grimaldi sat across from her, his back to the sliding glass doors leading to his outside patio. She noticed movement, somebody moving close and sidling around the fence separating her tiny patch of yard from his.

"How much?"

Camilla blinked at his words. "What?"

"How much will it take for you to look the other way while I quietly slip away?"

"I've got a better question, Mr. Grimaldi. What guarantee do I have you aren't going to have me killed the minute you walk away?" When he feigned shock, she shot back, "Don't try and play innocent. After your first attempt failed, you tried again. Did you put the rattlesnake in my bed yourself, or did one of your henchmen do it?"

"Should I pretend to know what you're talking about?" Grimaldi winced again when he straightened his leg, his hand rubbing the kneecap.

Camilla stood, giving Oscar a final pat. Time to finish, because she was tired. Tired of running. Tired of hiding. Sick and tired of having her life controlled by everyone— except her.

"Mr. Grimaldi, I'm not going to spend the rest of my life looking over my shoulder, knowing you're free and you've put a target on my back. Do you seriously believe I'm going to simply look the other way while you quietly slip out of the country, never paying for all the people you've killed, or had killed? I'm going to the police and telling them everything I know."

Grimaldi shook his head slowly, before struggling to his feet. Camilla drew in a long breath, noticing a second man poised outside, knew she was protected. Except she didn't expect Grimaldi to move so fast. Before she took a single step, he was on her, his hands wrapped around her throat, squeezing.

She struggled, clawing at his hands, choking with every breath before all air was cut off. Black spots appeared before her eyes and breathing grew harder and harder. Why weren't the people outside crashing through the glass to save her?

"You're not going to tell anybody anything, you stupid girl. And if you're waiting for the two men outside to come riding to your rescue, think again. They work for me. I'm never without men guarding my back." He squeezed tighter, his fingers digging into her throat.

Her last thought as she slipped into the blackness turned to Heath and how much she loved him.

Heath stood inside the van, positioned behind the man running the surveillance equipment. It was driving him crazy, knowing Camilla was inside with a killer, and he was stuck in the back of a van, twiddling his thumbs. There were several cars parked throughout the parking lot, with eyes on Grimaldi's townhouse.

"She's inside." Dandridge's low voice came from beside him, but Heath tuned him out. The only thing he wanted was to hear Camilla's voice, know she was okay, and then getting her out of Dodge.

Suddenly, the silence in the van was broken by the sound of Camilla's voice. Nothing special, the normal chitchat you'd expect between neighbors. His breath tightened in his chest when he heard Grimaldi's voice, remarking on Camilla's amnesia. He sounded surprised that she'd gotten her memories back, which was the plan.

Camilla played her part perfectly, a little bit innocent, a little taunting, deliberately keeping Grimaldi off balance. Too bad they'd been unable to get video along with the audio.

There. Grimaldi admitted his identity. "Isn't that enough? She's got him to admit he's Johnny Grimaldi. He didn't deny taking the shot at her. What more do you want?"

"Calm down, Boudreau. Let Ms. Stewart keep talking. The more he admits, the more evidence we'll have to prosecute. She's surrounded by cops. Nobody's going to hurt her."

"You'd better pray you're right."

Heath kept listening, detecting the subtle hint of fear in her voice. His stomach clenched, and he fought the urge to jump from the van, break through Grimaldi's door, and take him down. Camilla had to be safe. He wouldn't— couldn't—accept anything else.

"Boss, Grimaldi said he's got two bodyguards around back. He's made an active threat. Listen."

Dandridge grabbed his arm when Heath lunged for the van's door. "Stop. You can't go off half-cocked."

The sound of a struggle came through the mic. That was more than enough for Heath. Shaking off Dandridge's grip, he flung open the van's back door, and lunged out, hearing chaotic sounds behind him. He didn't care what they did, he needed to get to Camilla. The sound of shouted commands and running footsteps echoed around him, but he ignored them. Camilla needed help. She needed him.

When the doorknob didn't open beneath his hand, he backed up and rammed his foot against the door, which moved but didn't open. At his second kick, the doorjamb splintered, and the door flew inward. Reaching into the back of his waistband, he pulled his gun, and rocketed to a stop when he saw Grimaldi, his hands wrapped around Camilla's throat, squeezing tighter and tighter.

Camilla's fingers clawed at Grimaldi, but she was clearly losing the battle, her breathing shallow, her face a mottled red. Heath let loose a roar, and Grimaldi caught Camilla's body, which started to slump. He wrapped an arm around her waist, his other hand captured her throat, squeezing.

"Let her go." Heath bit out the words, his jaw clamped tight, and pointed his gun, sighting right between Grimaldi's eyes. An eerie calm centered deep inside, until all he saw was Camilla in Grimaldi's arms. In the background he heard shouting, even heard the muffled cries of the bodyguards as they were taken out by the cops. Who cared? All he wanted was Camilla safe.

"Back off, Boudreau, or I'll snap her neck."

A red haze colored Heath's vision, a boiling rage building deep in his gut. Grimaldi was a dead man. He might not be the one who pulled the trigger, but everything inside him screamed for Grimaldi to take his last breath. Though not until Camilla was free from his clutches.

"You know you're never walking out of this townhouse.

There's a SWAT team outside your door. The bodyguards you had stationed in the back have been incapacitated. The Feds will be here any second. Give yourself up without hurting Camilla, and maybe they'll be lenient."

"Keep dreaming. We both know the only way I'm leaving this place is in a body bag. Might as well take her," he shook Camilla's limp body roughly, "with me, since she's the busybody who's ruined everything."

"Camilla doesn't have anything to do with the situation you find yourself in, Grimaldi. You've left a trail of bodies between here and New York. You should have left the country while you had the chance."

Heath caught the slight rise and fall of Camilla's chest, and gave silent thanks she was still breathing. Grimaldi's hand around her throat had shifted when he'd caught her unconscious body against his. He was almost happy she'd passed out, not having to deal with the insanity gleaming in Grimaldi's eyes. The man had gone round the bend, which made him even more dangerous.

His gaze cut to the sliding glass door, and he nearly laughed aloud at what, or rather who, stood silhouetted on the other side. Uncle Gator held a hunting knife in one hand, his other reaching for the door handle. The back patio area had been cleared of the bodyguards, and a sole SWAT officer stood beside the fence, weapon at the ready, though he deferred to Gator as lead. Gator raised a finger to his lips in a shushing motion. Heath nodded, barely moving his head.

"Leaving the country wasn't an option before. Everything was laid out, going according to plan. I was lying low for another six months or so, waiting for the high-pressure search to die down. Then I was driving down to Florida and taking a charter boat to the Bahamas. From there, I'd fly to South America with nobody the wiser. Until this fool and her camera screwed everything up."

Grimaldi's face twisted up in a grimace of pain, and he gritted his teeth on his final words. Heath couldn't help noticing how pale and sallow his complexion appeared. A bead of sweat peppered his forehead, and his eyes looked glassy. He struggled to keep Camilla upright in his arms, and Heath wondered how much longer the other man could hold out.

"What's the big deal with the photo? It's not like Camilla was going to show it to anybody. It was simply a picture of a dog; your face barely shows. Nobody would have seen it."

"When I realized she'd taken my photo, I couldn't take any chances. I needed that picture gone. That one photo could ruin all my plans for getting out of the country."

"You figured if you shot her, it would be enough distraction for you to steal her phone with nobody the wiser. They'd assume whoever tried to carjack her stole her phone, right? Except you screwed up, because Camilla doesn't own a car, which screwed up your whole Good Samaritan act, because there was no outside party to blame. You knew sooner or later the cops would be back around, asking more questions, and somebody would recognize you."

"Who doesn't own a car nowadays? Even I have a car. Not in my real name, but still..."

Grimaldi's voice caught at the end of his sentence, and he drew in a ragged breath. Heath took a step forward and froze when Grimaldi's hand tightened around Camilla's throat again. From the corner of his eye, he saw the slider open a couple of inches, just enough for his Uncle Gator to squeeze through. Knew he had to create enough of a distraction for him to make his move.

"What now, Grimaldi? There's no place to run. No place to hide. Give Camilla to me, and you have my word I'll talk to the cops. I'll tell them you cooperated, willingly released the hostage. Heck, I'll even testify if you go to trial."

Grimaldi shook his head. "Can't take that chance, Boudreau. Tell the cops..." His words cut off abruptly, his eyes widening in shock. Heath spotted the light glittering off the shiny knife that appeared like a ghost pressed tight against Grimaldi's throat. Gator stood behind him, his hand wrapped securely around the knife.

"Very gently give Ms. Stewart to Heath. No tricks. You even twitch and my hand might slip." Gator's voice was barely above a whisper as he leaned in close, speaking in Grimaldi's ear. Heath doubted the mic Camilla wore would pick up the words. He hoped so; he really wanted to keep Gator out of this mess if possible.

Grimaldi swallowed, his Adam's apple bobbing dangerously close to the knife's edge. "Who are you?"

"I'm your worst nightmare, and I'll haunt you forever if you hurt a single hair on Ms. Stewart's head. Do what I said, give her to Heath."

"Okay, okay. Boudreau, take her."

Heath stepped forward, sliding his arms around Camilla, and lifting her up and away from Grimaldi, who seemed to collapse inwardly on himself. A quick tap on the temple from the butt end of Gator's knife and he slid to the floor.

"She okay?"

Camilla gave a soft sigh, and turned her head into his shoulder, and Heath finally drew the first easy breath since he'd burst through the front door. "She's going to be fine. You'd better go, before the cops come in, unless you want to get caught up in this."

"I'll be close. Call me."

"I will." Heath heard commotion heading up the front walk. "Go. I'll handle the police."

Without a word, Gator slipped out the back, pausing only long enough to talk to the officer stationed by the fence, who gave a sharp nod. He remained a silent sentry, even as Gator disappeared.

Chaos erupted, with cops and Feds swarming into the apartment, guns drawn. Heath left them to deal with the fallout, since Grimaldi wasn't going anywhere. He had more important things to deal with. Like taking care of the woman he loved.

CHAPTER TWENTY-ONE

"I can't believe Grimaldi's dead."

"Dandridge claims it was a heart attack. I've gotta say, I'm not surprised. He had trouble breathing when I confronted him. Pale and sweaty. Still, I'm not feeling overly sympathetic a crazed serial killer got his just desserts."

Camilla laid the pizza box in the middle of the table and grabbed a couple of bottles of water from the fridge. Since there wasn't any food in the house, Heath called for a pizza delivery, insisting she eat. He refused to leave, even for a second, though half a dozen police officers were right next door, going over the crime scene with a fine-toothed comb.

Reaching overhead into the cupboard, Camilla pulled down a bowl and poured some water for Oscar. When the authorities told her the dog would likely end up at the pound, it nearly broke her heart. Besides, he deserved a lot of the credit. Without him, Grimaldi might never have been caught. Bending down, she scratched him behind the ears, giving him a little extra loving. He was a cute little thing, barely two pounds, but a little ball of energy.

"I can't believe it's finally over. No more looking over

my shoulder or running for my life. Grimaldi dropping dead of a heart attack seems a bit anticlimactic."

Heath snorted. "I doubt the Feds or the cops feel that way. More like closure of multiple years of seeking justice for the families of the people Grimaldi killed. Their biggest question right now is what he did with the millions in diamonds he absconded with when he first disappeared. They haven't got a clue where he hid them."

"Really?" Camilla chuckled and took a bite of her pizza, closing her eyes as the tomato and cheese flavors burst across her tongue. She hadn't realized how hungry she was. "Tell them to check his cane."

"His cane?" Heath tilted his head, studying her intently.

"Uh-huh. Think about it. Guy never let it out of his sight, carried it everywhere. It is the perfect hiding place, and he had a legitimate excuse for carrying it, because of the leg injury. Bet it's hollow, and the diamonds are inside. As an added bonus, if he had to hit the road unexpectedly, he had the stones available instantly. It's actually kind of brilliant."

Heath laid his slice down, pulled out his phone and quickly dialed. "Hey, Dandridge, Camilla said to check Grimaldi's cane. She thinks that's where he kept the diamonds. Yeah, I'll hold." Heath winked at her, and Camilla bit back her chuckle. She loved how he could make her laugh without even trying.

"He's looking?"

Heath nodded and grabbed his water, taking a long swallow, the phone still to his ear. "Yeah, I'm here. Really? That's good news. I'll let her know. Absolutely, I'll call you," he added and hung up.

"Was I right?"

"Yep. Dandridge says you get a gold star and can work with him anytime."

"I think I'll stick with writing about suspense. Living it isn't nearly as much fun."

They ate in companionable silence, and Camilla tossed a piece of crust onto her plate and rolled her neck, giving a contented sigh. This was nice. Being able to take a relaxing break, and not worry about anything except simply being with Heath. Only now the danger was past, he'd probably head back to D.C.

"Ready to talk?"

"I guess."

Heath held out his hand and helped her stand, leading her to the living room. She sank down onto the sofa, curling her legs beneath her, dreading the upcoming conversation. Things had to go back to normal, and he'd be heading back to his job with the ATF. She'd return to her lonely life, isolated from everybody and everything, alone with her computer and her stories. But she loved him enough to let him go. She'd always remember he'd said he loved her, but that confession had been in the heat of the moment.

"I have to head back to D.C. in the morning, sweetheart." He slid onto the sofa beside her and rested his arm along its back. "I've used up pretty much all the vacation time I've got on the books, and they're expecting me."

"I understand, I really do. You'll never know how much I appreciate everything you've done for me. I'm not sure I could have handled things without you. You—you saved my life." She gave him a watery smile, fighting the tears threatening to spill. "I will never forget what you've done. If you ever—"

His brow scrunched, lips curved into a frown. "What are you talking about? You're acting like we'll never see each other again."

"We won't. I mean, we might run into each other at the Big House if you're there when I visit Beth and Jamie, but—"

"Cam, did you mean it when you said you love me?"

Her heart seized in her chest. How could he ask her that? She'd all but laid herself bare, admitting her feelings. Taking a deep breath, she confessed, "Of course I meant it. Every word. I love you with my whole heart and soul, and it's breaking me to say goodbye."

"I love you, Cam. You are my heart, my soul. I have no intention of saying a permanent goodbye, ever." When his hand cupped her cheek, the tears she'd been fighting spilled over, trailing down her cheeks. He gently wiped them away, the warmth in his eyes causing her breath to catch in her throat.

"Really? But...I thought...how are we going to make this work? I know D.C. isn't an insurmountable distance, but long-distance relationships aren't easy. Most of the time they don't work. I don't want us to fail."

"And we won't. I wanted to ask, how do you feel about living in Texas?"

Something broken inside her blossomed with hope. The most lovely feeling of warmth swept through her, unlike anything she'd ever felt before.

"I like Texas, especially if you're talking Shiloh Springs. Why?"

The corners of his lips kicked up, his smile accentuating the twinkle in his blue eyes. "I'm going to request a transfer as soon as I get back to work. No guarantees it'll happen, and I'd have to work out of Austin, because there's no ATF office in Shiloh Springs. I'd have to live there, but it's close enough we could visit everyone all the time. What do you think?"

"I don't—are you asking me to move to Texas?"

"No."

"I...oh, okay. Sorry, I jumped to the wrong—"

"Camilla Stewart, I love you. You love me. I don't want to spend a single minute without you in my life. No, I'm not asking you to move to Texas. Well, yes, I am, but not in the way you're thinking. I want you to live with me and love me until eternity and beyond. I want you to be my friend, my lover, and my everything. Marry me?"

"Yes! Oh, Heath, yes!"

His lips crashed against hers, and she poured all her love into the kiss, telling him without further words how she adored him, and wanted to spend the rest of her life with him. The man who'd teased and tormented her from the day they'd met, the man she loved, and would love until her last breath pulled her close against him, deepening their kiss.

Heath Boudreau was the man of her dreams, and she couldn't wait to spend the rest of her life on the wild and crazy ride of her lifetime with the man who'd stolen her heart.

Laissez le bon temps rouler!

CHAPTER TWENTY-TWO
EPILOGUE

Shiloh scanned the e-mails on his laptop, only half paying attention. As tired as he felt, he couldn't get his brain focused on anything but Renee O'Malley. Or the woman they assumed was Lucas' long lost sister. He'd gotten so close tonight. Close enough he could've reached out his hand and touched her. Until something or someone spooked her, and his gut screamed it was him.

Scaring her was the last thing he intended. He'd spent years knowing about her, wondering about her, and now he'd gotten closer to finding her than ever. Nothing would keep him from finally reuniting her with Lucas.

When his cell phone rang, he answered without bothering to look at the caller ID.

"How's my baby?"

"Hello, Momma. I'm good. How's everything at home?"

"Everybody's fine. Sorry I'm calling so late, but I was thinking about you, and needed to hear your voice. Now, tell me why haven't I gotten an update on Renee? You're in Portland looking for her, and I had to find out from somebody else. Why's that, hmm? I get the feeling y'all are hiding something. Your Dad's all closemouthed, Lucas...well, he's being Lucas. He's not getting his hopes up, after so many close calls. And I'm tired of being left out of the loop when it comes to finding Renee."

Shiloh squirmed on the chair, like he'd always done as a kid when his mother got *that* tone in her voice. She had a way of making him feel guilty, even when he hadn't done anything wrong. Probably a trick all mothers knew; a trade secret they passed along to one another at tea parties.

"Can't blame Lucas. The last couple of years, it seems like one step forward and two steps back in his search for her. I think it's eating at him—the guilt. He got the best deal possible, under trying circumstances. Living with the Boudreaus must've seemed like a dream come true to a kid whose whole world had disintegrated before his eyes. I can't imagine what life would've been like if I hadn't had Ridge. And you. He doesn't know how Renee grew up, whether she had a happy, loving home or if her life was a nightmare."

"Trust me, son, we were the lucky ones. Having you and your brother join our family was one of the happiest days of my life. Now, tell me what you've found out."

Shiloh leaned back and rubbed a hand across his face. He didn't want to tell his mother too much and get her hopes up. On the other hand, he wasn't about to lie to her either. Patti Boudreau had the uncanny ability to detect a lie at a hundred yards, especially if uttered by one of her sons.

"I'm getting close. While I'm not one hundred percent positive, I honestly believe the woman calling herself Elizabeth Reynolds is Renee O'Malley, Lucas' sister. I got a good look at her tonight, and she looks enough like him I'm convinced."

"You saw her? Why didn't you talk to her?"

Shiloh winced at the hopefulness in his mother's voice. She'd embrace Renee without question and make her a part of the Boudreau clan. Heck, as far as all the Boudreaus were concerned, Renee was family; she just didn't know it yet.

"Sorry, Momma. I wasn't quite close enough, and she slipped away. But I'm going back to her apartment tomorrow, and I'll keep searching. I'm not giving up until I find her."

"Don't you have other cases you need to work? Maybe one of your brothers can go to Portland and—"

"No! I've got this. My schedule's clear, and my partner can handle anything while I'm here."

"Alright, but if you need anything, I'm always here." She paused before adding, "I miss you. I know, I know, San Antonio isn't far, but it's not the same as you being home. I miss having all my boys living close. By the way, did your Daddy tell you Heath's moving back? He'll have to get a place in Austin for his job, but I'll find him and Camilla a place here in Shiloh Springs, too, so they can come home most weekends."

"Really? I haven't talked to him in a bit. Did you say

Camilla's moving with him? Sounds like I missed a lot."

His mother chuckled, the sound like soothing music to Shiloh. "He and Camilla had quite an adventure. You know she got shot, right? Anyway, he brought her to the Big House, and sent your Uncle Gator to Charlotte. Told him to snoop around and see if he could uncover who'd shot her."

Shiloh let out a low whistle. Heath mentioned the last time they'd spoken he'd recruited Uncle Gator. His uncle was part bloodhound and part alligator, like his namesake. Both animals epitomized the man; the bloodhound wouldn't give up on the scent, and the alligator would latch on and never let go.

"I know you're dying to tell me what happened, Momma. Did they figure it out?"

"You'll never believe it. Camilla's next door neighbor turned out to be a mobster, part of some New York or New Jersey syndicate family. Apparently, he was on the run with millions of dollars of diamonds. Plus, he was a wanted killer to boot. Since his face was on every watch list, he couldn't simply up and leave the country. Turns out, he disguised himself as a little old man, and moved into the townhouse next to Camilla."

"That's quite a coincidence. How'd they figure it out?"

"That's the fun part. Destiny—you know your brother's computer expert—she went digging on Camilla's phone and found a picture Camilla took of the guy with his dog. Recognized him immediately, and did some kind of voodoo with a facial recognition program. After that, Camilla came up with a plan to trap the guy into confessing to being the one who shot her."

Shiloh shook his head, marveling at the excitement in his mother's voice. Sounded like she was living vicariously through Heath and Camilla's adventure. "I'm dying to know, who was this guy?"

"Ever heard of Johnny 'The Chain' Grimaldi?"

Shiloh choked on the soda he'd just drunk, spewing it all over his shirt. "Are you kidding? Guy's been in the news for months. He's suspected of killing multiple people. Camilla faced him down? Is she okay?"

"She's going to be fine. Her memories haven't come back, except bits and pieces, and the doctors don't think they will at this point, and she's resigned herself to never knowing all the details, now that Grimaldi can't hurt her. I'm sure you'll get all the gory details from Heath." His mother chuckled, before adding, "Camilla's one smart cookie. Tricked him into confessing he'd taken a shot at her, and got it on tape. Oh, and Grimaldi had a heart attack. He's dead. She even figured out where he hid the diamonds. Camilla's soft-hearted; she adopted Grimaldi's dog when she found out it'd end up at the pound. It's the cutest little Yorkie, such a tiny thing." Her laughter was contagious and Shiloh found himself smiling again at the sound.

"Please tell me you've got pictures of Heath with the little ball of fluff?" He was so going to razz his six foot five, two hundred and twenty pound brother about having an itty-bitty puppy.

"No making fun of your brother. He adores Oscar."

"Oscar? You're joking, right? Nobody names a dog Oscar. That's almost as bad as naming it Spot or Fido."

"Apparently they do. They're bringing the dog with them when they move back. Camilla's excited about living in Texas. Says she's getting all kinds of ideas for a brand new series about cowboys."

"She'll find lots of them around Shiloh Springs. Listen, Momma, I'm going to have to go. I need to get up early and see if I can catch up with Renee. I promise I'll call as soon as I have any news."

"You better. You might be too big to put over my knee, but I've become inventive as you boys have gotten bigger."

"I love you, Momma."

"Love you, too, Shiloh. Be careful. And bring Renee home."

Shiloh swiped his finger across the phone, ending the call. Leaning back, he clicked an icon in his laptop and studied the photograph that opened. A smiling face with long auburn hair and a twinkle in her jade green eyes filled the screen. The intelligence in her gaze spoke to him, and he leaned in closer to the screen, running a fingertip along her cheek.

"I'm not giving up, Renee. There's a whole family waiting to welcome you with open arms. You might've slipped through my fingers tonight, but I'm going to find you and bring you home. Where you belong."

Thank you for reading Heath, Book #6 in the Texas Boudreau Brotherhood series. I hope you enjoyed Heath and Camilla's story. I loved writing their book.

Want to find out more about private investigator *Shiloh Boudreau* and the excitement and adventure he's about to plunge headfirst into? Will he find Lucas' long-lost sister, Renee? Keep reading for an excerpt from his book, Shiloh, Book #7 in the Texas Boudreau Brotherhood. Available at all major e-book and print book stores.

SHILOH
(Book #7 Texas Boudreau Brotherhood series) © Kathy Ivan

LINKS TO BUY SHILOH:
www.kathyivan.com/Shiloh.html

S hiloh Boudreau stood close to the bar, nursing his bottle of water, and wishing he'd opted for a beer instead. Couldn't do that, though, because he was working. He scanned the crowd again, looking for his mark. Earlier he'd spotted the woman he sought easing through a door leading backstage. When he'd tried to follow, one of the club's security guards stopped him in his tracks.

So here he was, forced to cool his jets at the bar, waiting for her to reappear. Would she? The itch on the back of his neck, the one he got when something was about to happen, had the little hairs standing at attention. Acting on a hunch, because that's all it was, he slid the half-empty bottle onto the bar and headed for the exit. The minute he was through the front door, he sprinted toward the alley.

Son of a gun, I'm too late!

He watched the city bus pull away from the curb, saw her shining auburn hair highlighted in the interior lights, as she took a seat toward the back. *Too little, too late again.* He'd missed her by mere seconds. Somehow, some way, she managed to stay two steps ahead of him. If he didn't know better, he'd swear somebody tipped her off whenever he got close.

Too bad she didn't know who she was messing with. He was a Boudreau and they didn't know the meaning of giving up. If she thought he'd simply turn tail and head back to Texas, she'd didn't have a clue. This case wasn't about a paycheck. It was a family quest, and he'd promised his brother, Lucas, he'd find Renee. Long-lost sister, separated from Lucas when they were youngsters, and put into the foster care system.

Lucas had been one of the lucky ones. He'd been placed

at the Big House with the Boudreau clan. Renee simply disappeared into the foster care system, and all records pertaining to her were mysteriously lost.

He flinched when she gave him a jaunty wave as the bus pulled away. No way could he manage getting back to his car and catch up to the rapidly departing bus. Parking had been a bear, and he ended up finding a spot several blocks away from the club. Some P.I. he was, he hadn't even gotten the number off the bus to see what areas it covered.

Giving a heavy sigh, he started back for his car. Might as well head back to his hotel room, and get a good night's sleep, and start over in the morning. Renee O'Malley might be slicker than a greased piglet, but she'd find out soon enough she was dealing with a Boudreau. Giving up wasn't in his vocabulary, and he tended toward being tenacious as a bloodhound once he scented his prey.

NEWSLETTER SIGN UP

Don't want to miss out on any new books, contests, and free stuff? Sign up to get my newsletter. I promise not to spam you, and only send out notifications/e-mails whenever there's a new release or contest/giveaway. Follow the link and join today!

http://eepurl.com/baqdRX

REVIEWS ARE IMPORTANT!

People are always asking how they can help spread the word about my books. One of the best ways to do that is by word of mouth. Tell your friends about the books and recommend them. Share them on Goodreads. If you find a book or series or author you love – talk about it. Everybody loves to find out about new books and new-to-them authors, especially if somebody they know has read the book and loved it.

The next best thing is to write a review. Writing a review for a book does not have to be long or detailed. It can be as simple as saying "I loved the book."

I hope you enjoyed reading Heath, Texas Boudreau Brotherhood Book #6.

If you liked the story, I hope you'll consider leaving a review for the book at the vendor where you purchased it and at Goodreads. Reviews are the best way to spread the word to others looking for good books. It truly helps.

BOOKS BY KATHY IVAN

www.kathyivan.com/books.html

<u>TEXAS BOUDREAU BROTHERHOOD</u>
Rafe
Antonio
Brody
Ridge
Lucas
Heath
Shiloh (coming soon)

<u>NEW ORLEANS CONNECTION SERIES</u>
Desperate Choices
Connor's Gamble
Relentless Pursuit
Ultimate Betrayal
Keeping Secrets
Sex, Lies and Apple Pies
Deadly Justice
Wicked Obsession
Hidden Agenda
Spies Like Us
Fatal Intentions
New Orleans Connection Series Box Set: Books 1-3
New Orleans Connection Series Box Set: Books 4-7

CAJUN CONNECTION SERIES
Saving Sarah
Saving Savannah
Saving Stephanie
Guarding Gabi

LOVIN' LAS VEGAS SERIES
It Happened In Vegas
Crazy Vegas Love
Marriage, Vegas Style
A Virgin In Vegas
Vegas, Baby!
Yours For The Holidays
Match Made In Vegas
One Night In Vegas
Last Chance In Vegas
Lovin' Las Vegas (box set books 1-3)

OTHER BOOKS BY KATHY IVAN
Second Chances (Destiny's Desire Book #1)
Losing Cassie (Destiny's Desire Book #2)

ABOUT THE AUTHOR

USA TODAY Bestselling author Kathy Ivan spent most of her life with her nose between the pages of a book. It didn't matter if the book was a paranormal romance, romantic suspense, action and adventure thrillers, sweet & spicy, or a sexy novella. Kathy turned her obsession with reading into the next logical step, writing.

Her books transport you to the sultry splendor of the French Quarter in New Orleans in her award-winning romantic suspense, or to Las Vegas in her contemporary romantic comedies. Kathy's new romantic suspense series features, Texas Boudreau Brotherhood, features alpha heroes in small town Texas. Gotta love those cowboys!

Kathy tells stories people can't get enough of; reuniting old loves, betrayal of trust, finding kidnapped children, psychics and sometimes even a ghost or two. But one thing they all have in common – love and a happily ever after). More about Kathy and her books can be found at

WEBSITE: www.kathyivan.com

Follow Kathy on Facebook at facebook.com/kathyivanauthor

Follow Kathy on Twitter at twitter.com/@kathyivan

Follow Kathy at BookBub
bookbub.com/profile/kathy-ivan

CPSIA information can be obtained
at www.ICGtesting.com
Printed in the USA
LVHW080656090521
686869LV00017B/899

9 798578 020452